P9-BAW-521

Sun, Sand, Murder

Sun, Sand, Murder

JOHN KEYSE-WALKER

MINOTAUR BOOKS
NEW YORK

This is a work of fiction. All of the characters, organizations, and events portrayed in this novel are either products of the author's imagination or are used fictitiously.

www.minotaurbooks.com

Designed by Omar Chapa

Library of Congress Cataloging-in-Publication Data

Names: Keyse-Walker, John, author.
Title: Sun, sand, murder / John Keyse-Walker.
Description: First edition. | New York : Minotaur Books, 2016.
Identifiers: LCCN 2016010571 | ISBN 978-1-250-08829-1 (hardback) | ISBN 978-1-250-08830-7 (e-book)
Subjects: LCSH: Police—British Virgin Islands—Fiction. | Murder—Investigation—Fiction. | Anegada (British Virgin Islands)—Fiction. | Mystery fiction. | BISAC: FICTION / Mystery & Detective / Police Procedural.
Classification: LCC PS3611.E977 S86 2016 | DDC 741.5/973—dc23
LC record available at https://lccn.loc.gov/2016010571

Our books may be purchased in bulk for promotional, educational, or business use. Please contact your local bookseller or the Macmillan Corporate and Premium Sales Department at 1-800-221-7945, extension 5442, or by e-mail at MacmillanSpecialMarkets@macmillan.com.

First Edition: September 2016

10 9 8 7 6 5 4 3 2 1

To Irene, with love

Sun, Sand,
Murder

Prologue

Walking along the water's edge, the killer thought about the gun. Was bringing it the right thing to do? It was meant to frighten the man, to show him that this was serious business, to let him know that he could not cast someone aside so easily. There was a weight, a heft, to the gun in the bottom of the bag, and there was power in that weight. The killer needed the power the gun held. Yes, bringing the gun was right. The killer felt strong, and the gun multiplied that strength.

After a mile, the killer turned from the water and climbed the low dune. From the top, the man could be seen on the flat land below, still digging though it was late in the day. The man did not notice he wasn't alone until the killer was upon him, standing at the brink of the pit where the man bent with his shovel. The man was sweating but clean, the killer noticed, the white sand in which he dug not clinging to his shorts or his shirtless torso.

"I told you not to come back here," the man said. He boosted himself from the hole using the handle of the shovel, and, once up, he cast the shovel aside and placed his hands on his hips.

"We had an agreement," the killer said.

"I told you yesterday, the agreement's off."

"You can't do that to me."

The man laughed. "I can and I have."

"It's not that easy. Not with me," the killer began.

The man took a step forward and struck the killer against the side of the head with his fist. Ears ringing with the blow, the killer staggered and fell. The iron taste of blood spread across the killer's tongue; a tooth had cut the inside of the killer's cheek.

The man stood above as the killer reached into the bag and closed trembling fingers around the checked pistol grip. Drawing the gun and feeling its weight, the killer pointed the barrel up at the man and felt the power of the gun and the strength it gave.

"I am so tired of all this trouble with the help," the man said, and reached down for the gun.

The killer looked directly into the man's eyes and pulled the trigger. The man's eyes had no time to register fear, or surprise, before the .38 slug entered just above the bridge of his nose and tore off the back of his skull.

The killer rose slowly and gazed down at the body sprawled in the hot sand.

"You fucked with the wrong person," the killer said, and turned east to walk back along the beach.

As the killer crested the dune, the first of the land crabs scuttled toward the man's corpse.

Chapter One

I ran my hand along the smooth curve of Cat Wells's hip. Fine grains of sand adhered where she had rolled from the blanket as we made love. She dozed in the sun, or pretended to. I looked out across the placid waters of Windlass Bight and wondered how I had gotten myself into this mess. Living in a simple place does not always make for a simple life.

I suppose it wasn't truly a mess because no one knew Cat and I had been meeting in secluded spots around the island for the last six months. Icilda, my wife, neither knew nor suspected anything was amiss in our marriage. Icilda's daily routine of home and kids, waiting tables at the Reef Hotel, and any spare moments devoted to her activities at the Methodist church did not allow time for the detection of infidelity.

Not that she had any cause to be suspicious. I had been a model husband throughout our marriage. A good breadwinner, working three steady jobs and guiding on the side. A good father to our children, Tamia and Kevin. Always attentive to Icilda's needs and wants. Faithful throughout our twenty years together.

Until now. Now I was unfaithful, a cheater, a selfish lowlife, a dirtbag. I knew what I was doing could ruin my marriage and my family but try as I might I could not give Cat up, could not act with respect for my wife, could not honor my marriage vows.

I'm still not sure how my affair with Cat got its start. I know precisely when it all began; it is the "how" that seems so hard to grasp. The "when" was a fine September morning. I was to meet two anglers traveling from St. Thomas for a day of fly-fishing on the shallow bonefish flats that surround much of my home island, Anegada. My contact in St. Thomas told me the clients would be arriving at Captain Auguste George Airport on VI Birds Air Charters. The pilot was new to the Virgin Islands and both she and the clients would need to clear customs at the airport. This was not a problem, since, in addition to my other occupations, I am the customs officer for Anegada.

There were no other incoming flights scheduled for that morning. I arrived early and waited alone inside the one-room shed that serves as the airport terminal. HRH Queen Elizabeth II stared balefully down on me from the faded coronation portrait that had graced the terminal wall since the building's dedication. The southeast trade wind wafted through the open door. A hen and three black chicks searched for morsels along the edge of the gravel runway. Otherwise, nothing and no one seemed to be about.

A few minutes after the scheduled arrival time, the silence of the morning was broken by the approach of a helicopter from the southwest. I shielded my eyes from blowing dust as the mango-yellow VI Birds copter settled in the taxi area and its rotors wound down.

Cat Wells emerged from the pilot's seat, wearing an unplugged radio headset draped like a fur around her exquisite neck. She was certainly different from the other pilots who flew to Anegada, usually eager pups hoping to work their way up the ladder to a job with a commercial airline. Unlike the pups, Cat Wells had presence, the kind of presence that stops male conversation when she enters a room. She moved with purpose across the taxi area, lithe and professional in khaki pants and a crisp white shirt with captain's bars on its shoulders. Her flawless mahogany complexion and her regal bearing called Nefertiti to mind, astray by three millennia but still serene and self-assured. Seeing me standing in the terminal entrance, she approached with an extended hand.

"Hi. Are you the customs man?" Her eyes were the deep green of a mountain lake, a rare attribute in a black woman. Those eyes took in my faded and frayed constable shirt, worn shorts, and sandals with a look of disapproval. Well, perhaps "disapproval" is too strong a word; the look had more than a hint of pity mixed in. Like a mother inspecting a child who had dressed himself in his favorite outfit, again, for the fifth day in a row. A slow burn of embarrassment rose from my neck to my ears. I was thankful my dark skin did not betray the flush.

"I am the customs officer for Anegada, and a special constable on the Royal Virgin Islands Police Force." For a reason that I could not fathom, the reply was delivered in a formal parade-ground voice. I instantly felt like an ass.

Cat came smartly to attention, lifting her outstretched hand into a snappy military salute. "Yes, suh!" she replied, drill sergeant sharp.

I felt like a huge ass.

An up-at-the-corner grin flashed across her face. I laughed. She laughed, no girlish giggle, a woman's laugh, warm and full.

"Mary Catherine Wells," she said, introducing herself. She dropped her hand from the salute and extended it in greeting again.

"Teddy Creque. It is a pleasure to meet you, Ms. Wells." I shook her hand. She allowed it to linger in my grasp. An invitation?

"My friends call me Cat. You can call me Cat." The sly grin again.

I was barely able to compose myself enough to collect the clients and their fishing gear, stamp their passports, and load them into my battered Royal Virgin Islands Police Force Land Rover. As I backed out of the parking space, my eyes were drawn to the sway of Cat's hips as she strolled back to the helicopter. Her timing was impeccable as she glanced back and caught me looking. The grin appeared a third time, followed by a little wave. I was hooked like a bonefish.

After that first encounter, it seemed as if events took over. I was not the instigator but certainly a willing participant. Cat's imp grin evolved into a saucy smile. Her playful eyes developed a seductive spark. When she flew in with passengers or cargo, the banter between us was light, smart, and sexy.

She flew in one day a month after our first encounter with guests for the Reef Hotel. After they were met and driven away, she offered to share a thermos of coffee with me. We sat in the shade of the terminal shed and talked for an hour. She told me about growing up "everywhere" as an army brat, how the military was her family business, and how she had become a pilot and served in the Persian Gulf in Operation Desert Storm. My part in the conversation was a description of my work as a fishing guide and a few tales of life here on the island.

I told myself that it was just friendly and innocent, but we both knew what was crackling just below the surface of our conversation. We were on the brink of acting out the same play that had been acted out a million times since the first innocent man had a coffee with an innocent woman he had not told his wife about. I spent the entire drive back to The Settlement that day convincing myself that nothing had happened and nothing was happening.

The following week Cat flew in with a cargo of spare generator parts and a six-pack of Red Stripe. We drove to Windlass Bight with nary a word, drank the beer, and made love on a blanket in the shade of the sea grape trees.

Then I went home to Icilda and the kids. As Icilda made dinner, she complained about a rude customer at the hotel restaurant who had left no tip. Tamia whined for permission to go shopping with a friend on Tortola over the weekend. Kevin proudly showed off a report card with all Bs as his marks. It was like any normal night in the Creque household, except for Cat's gasps, and her ultimate exclamation, playing out in my memory as a background soundtrack to the evening. It was like any normal night, if a normal night included the searing guilt of betraying your wife and children.

So it had been for these past few months, once or twice every week. Cat and I had savored each other's bodies neck-deep in the clear waters of Bones Bight. We had hasty, half-clothed sex against the wall of the deserted airport terminal. She had rocked languidly atop me at Table Bay, the motion of her hips timed to the thunder of the surf against the offshore reef. It was not love, or even the shadow of love. Neither of us harbored that illusion. It was lust, pure and simple. We took sex hungrily from one another and did not ask many questions, of each other or of ourselves.

After each tryst, I returned to my life as if what had occurred had never happened. I went to my shift at the power plant and drowsed to the hum of the generator. I poled my skiff, the *Lily B*, a sweating Yankee fisherman on the bow platform, and strained to spot bonefish through the mirror surface of the water. I ran my police patrol around the dusty washboard tracks we call roads on Anegada, stopping at the Cow Wreck Beach Bar and Grill to show the sunburned tourists sipping rum drinks that they were safe, despite the fact that the nearest real RVIPF officer was miles away on Tortola. I saw to Icilda's carnal needs, with a detachment she did not seem to notice. Or at least care about.

I was leading two lives, one dull, ordinary, and filled with virtue, the second risky, clandestine, and exciting. I knew that I should stop seeing Cat. It was the right thing to do and it was the only way to extract myself from this undiscovered mess. It was the only way to recover some shred of my self-respect. I resolved time and time again to end the thing I had with her. Each time I failed, weak, never raising the topic, succumbing to her smile, to the uninhibited joy of being in her presence, the danger, and the need of my body to have hers.

Now she rolled toward me, waking and showing her mischievous grin. The day's unspoken vow to end our affair would remain unfulfilled. I stroked the back of her neck. She arched herself into my body.

"Teddy. Teddy. You there? Pick up." The aging CB in the Land Rover, the only sure means of communication on Anegada given the lack of cell phone service and the unwillingness of the bureaucrats in Road Town to invest in an actual police radio, carried the urgency in Pamela Pickering's voice.

"Teddy. Teddy. It's Pamela. Pick up, please!" Pamela is Anegada's administrator, the island's only public official other than me. The eldest child of Pinder Pickering, Anegada's first administrator, Pamela believes herself to be Anegada royalty. She inherited her position when Pinder's consumption of Heineken forced him to make his de facto retirement to the Reef Hotel bar official. On his most alcohol-clouded day, Pinder was ten times as competent as the lazy and disorganized Pamela.

"Teddy. Teddy. It's an emergency!" Pamela squawked. The last emergency call Pamela had made to me was when her car was out of gas and she was in danger of missing the ferry to Tortola. It was not the first occasion she had treated me as her personal servant, though she had no actual authority over me. I usually acceded to her "orders"; it was easier than arguing with her.

I rose from the blanket and reached in the window of the Land Rover. Cat followed and curled against me, sliding a hand ever so slowly down my groin.

I grabbed the CB microphone, overcoming the urge to grab Cat instead.

"This is Teddy. Switch to the alternate channel." Everyone on Anegada monitored channel 16 like a party telephone line. There was no need for the whole island to hear Pamela turn me into her private taxi for the second time in as many weeks.

I flipped to the alternate channel. "All right, Pamela. What is the emergency?"

"De Rasta here, Teddy, De White Rasta, an' he say he found a dead man out at Spanish Camp."

Chapter Two

Every child who attends the Anegada School learns that our island was discovered by Christopher Columbus on his second voyage to the New World in 1493. Columbus did not actually set foot on the island. The expedition's flagship, *Marigalante,* anchored offshore while a landing party in a small boat braved a gap in the Horseshoe Reef to come ashore in search of freshwater. The place where they landed is still called Spanish Camp, although Columbus recorded in his log that his men took only three hours to fill the ship's casks with "sweet water found in abundance" and did not even temporarily camp there. Life on Anegada has been fairly quiet since then.

The Admiral of the Ocean Sea exercised his naming prerogative as he passed through the neighborhood he called the Islands of Santa Ursula and the Eleven Thousand Virgins.

The hilly main island of the group became Tortola, Spanish for "Turtle Dove." The rocky island nearest to Anegada was christened Virgin Gorda, "Fat Virgin." The romance of naming the new lands had apparently vanished by the time he named the flat slab that is my home, Anegada, the "Drowned Land."

The great explorer got it right. While the other Virgin Islands, both US and British, are the summits of ancient mountains projecting above the sea, Anegada is a low-lying aberration. Its highest point is a sandbank that rises only thirty feet above the waters of Bones Bight. The eastern half of the island is a limestone shelf that an eon ago was part of the fringing Horseshoe Reef. The west is a sandbar built up on the canted limestone. Most of the interior is a rock and sand desert, harboring Antillean scrub thorn, squat cactus, century plants, and pygmy orchids that thrive in the blasting heat. No one goes into the interior except to cross to the beaches of the north and east shores.

Or to return from those beaches. Cat and I hurriedly packed up the Land Rover following Pamela's panicked call. The route to the police station in The Settlement took us past the airport. I dropped Cat off there, lingered only a moment to watch as she walked to her helicopter. Then I gunned the Land Rover over the washboard sand-and-limestone road toward town. I could only do forty miles per hour, jaws clenched against the jarring, while ducking low to keep my head from bouncing into the roof.

The Land Rover had a siren but I did not use it. I had never used it. The dozen or so vehicles on Anegada rarely encountered each other on the interior roads. The greater hazard on the road is the feral cattle. Descendants of the survivors of a cattle boat sinking in the 1930s, the skeletal cows, bulls, and calves move like molasses, unfazed by horns, shouts, or sirens. After maneuvering around a half dozen of the feeble beasts, I reached the lip of pavement marking the beginning of a quarter mile of concrete road and the outer boundary of Anegada's only town, if it can be called that, The Settlement.

The Settlement is where I grew up and where most of Anegada's two hundred souls live. There are no grocery stores, no pharmacies, no banks, and no fast-food restaurants there. Goats and chickens roam the sand lanes between small shacks baking in treeless yards marked by low limestone walls.

The closest thing to illicit entertainment is Cardi's Pool Hall, where the single snooker table with its shredded felt stands beneath a carport roof. On summer evenings, Anegada's young toughs gather there, boasting and posing in the manner of young toughs everywhere.

On Sunday morning, those same tough boys can be found at the island's only licit entertainment, the Methodist church, wedged with their siblings between Madda and Dada, singing hymns.

The same few families—the Faulkners, Pickerings, Vanterpools, Creques, Lloyds, and a handful of others—live, laugh, love, cry, and die in the same homes as generations of their ancestors before them. My parents still live in the same three rooms that at one time housed them, me, and my nine brothers and sisters in crowded chaos. I now live on the edge of town in a house I built the year before I married Icilda Faulkner, a four-room bungalow that most people in town view as striving and "putting on airs."

The four decades of my life have seen only two great changes in The Settlement. The first was the building of the power plant in 1977. The plant's two Caterpillar diesel engines standing on a concrete floor in a metal building supply Anegada's power needs on a somewhat intermittent basis tied to their age and state of repair. Jimmy Lloyd, Kevin Faulkner, and I split shifts as the plant operators. If the Caterpillars are working, it is a good opportunity to get eight hours of sleep. The construction of the power plant meant no more kerosene lanterns and stoves fired with torchwood gathered from the interior. There is actually a streetlight in The Settlement now. People have refrigerators. The blue light of television sets can be seen in some homes at night, with a satellite TV dish, that ultimate mark of civilization, perched atop the tin roof.

The second great change to The Settlement in my lifetime was construction of the Aubrey M. Vanterpool Administration Building and Community Center. In the spring of 1989, a small bulldozer, barged over from Tortola, clanked from the government dock up the main lane of The Settlement to push an acre clear of thorn and cactus. The next barge brought concrete blocks, a cement mixer, and a crew from the Department of Public Works, who constructed the only two-story building on the island, housing the police station and its never-used cell, our doctorless clinic, the single pickup truck of the fire brigade, and the administrator's office, where Pamela Pickering and De White Rasta awaited my arrival.

The limestone dust kicked up by the Land Rover's entry into the yard had not dissipated when Pamela Pickering, big hipped and wide eyed, erupted from the front entrance. She was followed closely by De White Rasta, as agitated as I had ever seen him. On this day, even his constant ganja high seemed insufficient to maintain his cool.

"Teddy, what you gon' do about the dead man out there?" Pamela gestured generally in the direction of Spanish Camp. De Rasta cringed behind her.

"I'm going to get some water and the clinic first aid kit and De Rasta and I are going to Spanish Camp to check it out."

The whites of De Rasta's bloodshot eyes grew wide and he gave an emphatic negative shake of his dirty blond dreadlocks. "Mon, I-mon not go back to where dat dead mon be lie-ens. I-mon nah go back deh ever again. Dat place fulla duppies."

I suspected the Rastafarian ghosts, the "duppies," that De White Rasta had seen had more to do with his cannabis intake than his eyesight. "Rasta, how will I find the man without you?" I reasoned.

"I-mon report as de law require. I done wit it."

"You black up today, Rasta?" I asked. I already knew the correct answer, "yes," as De White Rasta hardly missed an hour, let alone a day, without toking up. And I already knew the answer I would receive, an emphatic denial.

"No, mon. Why you fe galang so? I-mon don' touch de ganja. I-mon only smoke de shag. Ganja be illegal." The degree of De Rasta's indignation was matched only by the size of his lie. He burned more herb than a forest fire in Jamaica.

"If you haven't been smoking ganja, you didn't just imagine a dead man. If a man is dead, it could be foul play. Since you found the dead man, I have to treat you as a possible suspect. That means keeping my eye on you. So you can either come with me or I can lock you in the holding cell."

"Jah know I-mon nah harm de mon. Jah know I-mon go for a bit a peace an' quiet up dere an' just find dis mon. Sight? Why do dis to I, Teddy?" De Rasta whined.

"What will it be, Rasta?" I said, deciding further reasoning would be wasted effort.

De Rasta sighed a heavy sigh. "Okay, I and I go and I-mon show where de dead mon at. But dat all. I-mon not goin' in dat duppie place."

I went inside the police station and filled a plastic jug with water, put it in a backpack, and added the first aid kit from the clinic. When I came outside, De Rasta was lolling in the passenger seat of the Land Rover.

Pamela intercepted me on the way to the vehicle. "Shall I radio the deputy commissioner's office and let them know about the dead man?" Pamela's earlier panic had evolved into salacious excitement. Her eyes shone at the prospect of participation in an event that might be notable on Anegada for years to come.

"Wait until I see if there is anything to this. Who knows

what De Rasta has actually been smoking?" A flicker of disappointment crossed Pamela's face.

I eased the Land Rover through the gate and turned east, cruising slowly through The Settlement. In less than a minute we had traversed the paved road and continued onto the seldom-used sand path toward Spanish Camp. I turned toward De Rasta.

"Tell me exactly what you saw, Anthony. And cut the Rasta bull about duppies."

"Ghosts are as real as you and me, Teddy," De White Rasta said, his fake Jamaican patois replaced with an Eton-Oxford accent. I had heard De Rasta's speech undergo this transformation many times before but it still disconcerted me every time he made the verbal leap from Caribbean rustic to English aristocrat.

The first time De White Rasta had carried out his linguistic about-face for my benefit was when I was a neophyte special constable, commissioned for only six months. In one of the few communications my superior, the deputy commissioner, saw fit to make to me in two decades, I was warned of De White Rasta's impending arrival on Anegada. Specifically, I was told to expect "Anthony Wedderburn, white male, age twenty-two years, weight eleven stone, height five feet nine inches, eyes blue, hair blond, affects Rastafarian speech and appearance, including dreadlocks. Born Essex, UK. He is a frequent user of marijuana and has been expelled from a number of islands in Her Majesty's Commonwealth, most recently Barbados, without criminal charge. He is the son of a member of the House of Lords. His conduct is to be regulated so as to prevent harm to himself or others but is not otherwise to be interfered with."

In those days, as a brand-new special constable, I took myself and the job quite seriously. Consequently, I met Anthony Wedderburn two days after the message, when the fuel barge on which he had hitched a ride nudged up to the government dock at Setting Point. Carrying his worldly possessions in a burlap crocus bag, he stepped ashore smelling of ganja and goat, with a hint of diesel from his nap on the barge deck. His unfocused blue eyes drifted slowly left to right, then settled on my uniform shirt. "Big bout yah beef, I-mon yah brudda, no trouble," Anthony assured me. "Seen? I-mon shake out dis place soon. I-mon jus' a sufferer try'n to survive."

"Mr. Wedderburn, I am not your brother, any more than a white boy from Essex is a Rastafarian," I said. "But I am not here to make trouble for you. Anegada is a small place and we all need to get along. You won't have trouble from me if I don't have trouble from you."

The Rastafarian speech disappeared and De Rasta beamed a winning smile. "That is very sporting of you, old man. I plan only a short stay to take in the sights. You will have no trouble from me, because, you see, I am a friend to all mankind. I can assure you that you will not even know I am here." He shambled off the dock, looked both ways upon touching land, and randomly headed toward the West End.

Anthony Wedderburn had spent the years since that day drifting about the island, stoned on spliff and bothering no one. He ate what food he could cadge from belongers and tourists, wore cast-off clothing, and slept wherever he found himself at sunset. As the old millennium turned into the new, word arrived from London that his father had died. De White Rasta inherited the title of Lord Wedderburn, but he did not even leave for the funeral. I do not know where he got his ganja, but he never grew any on Anegada and never attempted to sell or give any to anyone here. At first we Anegadians made fun of him, naming him De White Rasta and joking about his appearance and speech, but he ultimately became a part of the fabric of our island life. He always spoke to everyone in his Rastafarian patois, except for me on those occasions when we were alone. I never let anyone here know of his origins.

"And if there were no ghosts at Spanish Camp before, the spirit of the poor devil I found out there this morning will certainly haunt the place from now on," De Rasta continued.

"What were you doing out at Spanish Camp?"

"Sometimes I sleep at Flash of Beauty."

Flash of Beauty was an old restaurant standing alone atop Loblolly High Point, with a stunning view of Loblolly Bay and the Atlantic beyond. Its owner had expected the dramatic location to draw tourists to snorkel in the pristine waters and eat local food made using authentic recipes. He was wrong. Most vacationers wanted a lounge chair on the closest beach, not a journey to Anegada's farthest corner. Despite the beauty of Flash of Beauty, it was now a tumbledown derelict on a forgotten beach. It was, however, the end point of the road closest to Spanish Camp.

"The breeze keeps the no-see-ums away at night," De Rasta explained. "I got up when the sun rose and noticed there were gulls circling and diving in the area of Spanish Camp. I thought it was probably jacks with a school of bait pushed up against shore, but I noticed there were no pelicans. I thought that was unusual and I had nothing better to do, so I walked down the beach toward the commotion. When I got closer, I could see the gulls were not by the shore at all. They were inland. That probably meant a dead cow, but as long as I had walked that far, I thought I might as well have a look."

De Rasta paused, took a deep breath, and then blew it out. "When I turned inland and got to the top of the sand dune, I saw what the gulls were after. Below the dune, maybe a hundred yards toward the salt pond, was a man. Or, I should say, a man's body. I knew it was a body because, even at that distance, you could see that the gulls had been at him pretty badly."

"Did you check the body?"

"No, I couldn't bring myself to go any further."

"Why not? The man could still be alive."

"Trust me, Teddy, he was not alive. And then there were the graves." De Rasta paled.

"Graves?"

"The man was surrounded by dozens and dozens of open graves."

Chapter Three

The uneven path to Loblolly Bay smoothed as we approached Flash of Beauty. The restaurant building, once painted gaudy green, yellow, and red, had now faded to a pale pastel smudge. Storms and vandals had broken the glass out of all its windows. The place had a shipwreck air about it.

Parking behind the building, De Rasta and I stepped around into the fresh breeze of the bay, a pleasant contrast to the interior of the island. Succulent plants dotted the sand slope down to the high-tide mark. A swath of the purest white sand extended from there to the modest surf. As the water deepened from the surf zone to the broken crust of the Horseshoe Reef, its color changed from clear white, to pale green, to emerald, to sky and then royal blue, and finally to purple-black in the depths outside the reef. The outer edge of the reef at Loblolly Bay marks the beginning of the

Anegada Trench, a two-mile-deep chasm, home to humpback whales and white marlins, and the start of the open sea. Sail east from there and the next landfall is Africa.

"The birds are still there." De Rasta pointed southeast along the beach. I could barely make out a cloud of minuscule dots, wheeling in the dazzling sun. In the near distance, a set of footprints trailed off toward the birds. The tide was falling, half out already.

"What time did you leave the beach for The Settlement, Anthony?"

"It was almost three-quarter tide, incoming." I had never seen De Rasta wear a watch, so the measure of time in his answer came as no surprise. It had been over four hours since he had started for help.

"Did you see anyone else around?" The obvious question, but I had not asked it before.

"I saw no one before I arrived at The Settlement, not here or on the road. Someone had been here, though. There were two sets of footprints when I went down the beach, a set going south and a set of the same coming back north. Bare feet, no shoes. They were small prints, a woman or a small man. The tide must have washed them away."

If the owner of the small footprints had walked from the water to the top of the sandbank near Flash of Beauty, it was not noticeable. The wind and the soft sand away from the water made any prints indistinguishable from those made by wild cattle last night or last week's adventurous tourist seeking seclusion for some naturist sunbathing. There were numerous car and truck tire prints near where we had parked, all equally indistinct.

"Come on, Anthony." I shouldered the backpack and started down the beach. De Rasta fell in at my side with a sigh. Twenty minutes walking at a quick pace brought us to a point seaward of the cloud of diving gulls.

De Rasta stopped and seated himself in the sand. "I am not going back to that graveyard, not now or ever again."

I was about to remonstrate but decided it was, after all, my job from here on out. I turned inland, climbing the gentle incline rising away from the beach. Lizards rustled in the dried seaweed as I walked. Waves collided with the reef offshore, their rumble like thunder on the cloudless morning.

The east trade wind was more vigorous when I crested the high dune. From the top, it was possible to see all the way across the island to the roofs of The Settlement and the green hump of Virgin Gorda beyond. The inland side of the dune was a carpet of low sea grape trees, divided by cow paths. Further downslope, the sea grapes tapered off to a dry salt pond. Bare limestone slabs poked above the thin soil in places. Fifty yards away, a clot of gulls squabbled over the torso of a man.

Even at that distance, I knew that the first aid kit I carried would not be needed. The body sprawled near a backpacker tent pitched on a level sandy patch. An area the size of a cricket field surrounding the tent was pocked with dozens of excavations that gave the appearance of being open graves. Each was a trench slightly wider than a man, as long or longer than a man is tall, and waist-deep. A mound of sand and broken limestone stood at the side of each hole. Whoever was doing the digging had not taken the time to refill any of the holes.

On the leeward side of the sandbank, the still air throbbed with the iron heat of a foundry. The white sand burned incandescent in the sun. As I approached the body of the man, the smell of baked flesh, not really rotten, stopped me. It was almost as if the corpse were cooking in the heat.

My life had been relatively free from contact with the dead to this point. My parents and near relatives are all alive. My grandparents were dead and gone before I was out of my infancy. The few funerals I had attended in The Settlement were closed-coffin. The isolated and peaceful lifestyle of Anegada meant that I had not encountered the dead at accidents or crime scenes in my duties as special constable. In short, nothing had prepared me for what I confronted at Spanish Camp.

The gulls retreated but the body seemed to squirm and almost levitate as I approached. Hundreds of crabs swarmed over the corpse, dissecting it as they fed. A land crab the size of a green coconut sidled away with a pinkie finger that had been clipped off at the first joint. Hermit crabs as small as a dime consumed shreds of flesh torn loose by the gulls.

Unlike the gulls, the crabs would not withdraw from their feast. I waded into the crawling mass, shouting and kicking them away. For many nights afterward, I had horrible nightmares populated by wave after relentless wave of crabs, green, brown, red, and remorseless, their black eyes impassive as they swarmed over my home.

I immediately recognized that the gulls and crabs had been consuming the remains of Paul Kelliher, PhD, of Boston University.

Professor Kelliher was well-known on Anegada. Rumor had it that he was a renowned herpetologist, a skilled academic politician, and a master obtainer of grants. For each of the last five winters, while his colleagues in Boston suffered through another season of slushy frozen agony, Professor Kelliher had come to sunny Anegada to study the habits of the endangered Anegada rock iguana. Our indigenous lizard is the size of a cocker spaniel and tastes like chicken, if chicken were covered in gray-green scales. I know this because people here hunted them for food until the few remaining members of the species retreated to the most inaccessible parts of the island. The remote localities where the few rock iguanas remain were where Professor Kelliher spent most of his time. He made only an occasional return to civilization to partake in a three-day bender at the Cow Wreck Beach Bar and Grill. It was not unusual for the professor to disappear into the wild for two or three weeks at a stretch. I rarely encountered him other than at Cow Wreck.

But here he was now, on his back in the hot sand. A gull had pecked away one of his eyes. His other eye stared blankly at the sun. Most of both his ears had been torn away by the crabs. His arms, spread like those of Jesus on the Cross, terminated in nubs where the fingers had been. He wore a pair of old Nikes, which had probably saved his toes from the crabs; a pair of khaki shorts, which had probably saved his privates; and nothing else.

There was a bullet entrance wound in his forehead, clean and neat as a widow's parlor. The bullet had angled upward, taking a huge chunk of the rear of his skull with it when it exited. The missing portion of the skull, like the many other missing parts of Professor Kelliher, had been spirited away by the local fauna.

I suddenly felt queasy and vomited my breakfast onto the sand an arm's length away from what remained of the professor's head. So much for crime scene integrity. The loss of breakfast helped me focus. I realized I had much to do and little to help me accomplish my duties.

I scanned the surrounding area. There were footprints by the hundreds, all made indistinct by the softness of the sand and the parade of crabs to and from the body. There were no guns, knives, ropes, lead pipes, wrenches, candlesticks, or other objects in the form of ready clues nearby.

I walked the few feet to the backpacker tent and peered inside. A pile of sandy bedding was mounded in the center of the floor. Rumpled clothing spilled out of a pack in one corner. A large jug of water and a handful of energy bars were the only supplies evident. The tent's contents were in disarray but it was impossible to tell whether they had actually been disturbed or if this was just the way Kelliher kept house.

I moved to look into one of the excavations. There was only time for a quick glimpse, as my movement away from the body was taken by the gulls and crabs as an invitation to return to the feast. There was a shovel beside the hole, which had been dug waist deep. The digger had gone on until he had encountered a layer of limestone. It did have the appearance of a shallow open grave. It could also have been the work of an ambitious kid playing in the sand. It just depended on the inclination of your mind.

It suddenly registered that this was my first crime scene. I decided I needed help, which meant I needed to call RVIPF headquarters in Road Town on Tortola. But first I had to do what I could to prevent the crabs and gulls from continuing their banquet.

In my four weeks of training to become a special constable, less than an hour had been devoted to how to deal with a body at a crime scene. The essence of the training was to preserve the situation as it was found and call in the real police. Calling the real police in the current circumstances meant a trek back to Flash of Beauty and leaving the body alone. I did not see De White Rasta as capable of providing any assistance, given his fear, authentic or sham, of "duppies." Besides, the idea was to keep civilians away from the crime scene, not bring them in to guard it. Sending De Rasta back while I stayed was not an option either. I had never seen him drive and did not know if he could operate the CB radio in the Land Rover.

I thought about covering the body with bedding taken from the tent. That would keep the gulls away but the crabs would not be deterred. A crab after carrion is as single-minded as a dog in heat. I could bury the body in one of the open holes, but that would involve moving it a fair distance and contaminating it with sand and dirt. I chose the middle course, dragging the corpse by the legs to the nearby tent and rolling it inside.

The open head wound smacked my arm as I folded the professor through the tent flap, leaving muculent bits of brain in its wake. The roasting-meat smell was immediately overpowering in the confined space. I zipped the tent closed and deposited the remainder of my stomach contents just outside the tent's threshold. Despite the heat, the sweat on my forehead was clammy and cold. I sat down in the sand and took some deep breaths. Maybe I was not made for police work after all.

Retracing my steps to the beach, I found De White Rasta seated with his feet in a tide pool, several broken sea urchins nearby.

"In all the excitement, I missed breakfast," De Rasta said. He gave me a cheery smile and offered an open urchin from which he had scooped half the roe. "I will gladly share this one with you, Teddy."

I gagged back my stomach's response to his offer, narrowly avoiding my third upchuck in an hour.

"Kelliher, the American, is dead back there." I gestured over my shoulder.

"What happened? Heart attack? Fall?"

"Not unless he fell forward onto a bullet. We have to get back to the Land Rover and call Road Town."

Neither of us spoke as we covered the mile back to Flash of Beauty. Violent death, even on a sublimely sunny day, can have that effect.

The difficulties of the day continued. I was unable to reach RVIPF headquarters on the low-powered CB radio. I ended up asking Pamela Pickering to relay a message by telephone. Lord knows what she told headquarters but she radioed back that I should be at the government dock in two hours to meet the *St. Ursula,* the RVIPF's only police vessel, bringing in the deputy commissioner and personnel from the Scenes of Crime Unit.

Chapter Four

Royal Virgin Islands Police Force deputy commissioner Howard Tuttle Lane stood in the bow of the *St. Ursula* as it approached the government dock, striking the same pose as George Washington crossing the Delaware. The deputy commissioner projected a gravitas that made the Father of the United States look like an unkempt slouch. A rigid six and a half feet tall, broad-shouldered and rock-solid, Deputy Commissioner Lane seemed to have skipped diapers and been born in navy blue uniform pants and a pressed khaki shirt. A round uniform hat, bearing the trademark navy and white checked hatband of the RVIPF, covered his shaved head and added to his altitude and dignity. His insignia of rank, badge, and belt buckle were polished to a high gloss. His flawless blue-black skin seemed to absorb the light reflected from the waters of Setting Point. He was off the boat in a single stride as the police officer behind the wheel cut the engine and glided to the government dock.

I stepped forward to greet the deputy commissioner, saluting-fingers together, palm out, as I had been taught twenty years before at the Regional Police Training Centre in Barbados.

I do not have much occasion for saluting on Anegada. In fact, the last time I had saluted was the day I received my appointment as special constable. The last man I had saluted that day was Deputy Commissioner Lane. After returning to headquarters in Road Town following the academy graduation ceremony, the DC had met with me in his office and given me the keys to the police station on Anegada. He had also provided a stern lecture about my being the only police presence on the island, even though, as he put it, special constables were "not real police officers," and how I was to be "the only civilization and order in that otherwise wild place." He concluded by handing me a small piece of paper with the combination to the police station safe and, reaching into his desk drawer, pulled out a Webley Mark III revolver. He released the break-top mechanism, opened the chamber, and eyed it to make certain it was not loaded. Snapping it shut, he handed it to me butt first. Heavy as a brick, the old gun had "HM West Indies Police Force 1932" stamped on the receiver. Spots of rust decorated the barrel.

"As you are so far removed from any assistance, I think you should have this. The regulations say special constables are not to be armed, but with no regular police officer on

Anegada, I am making an exception to the regulations." The DC's sober gaze was more disquieting than the pistol in my hand. He handed me a box of .38/200 shells. "Put it in the safe, Special Constable, and do not take it out unless someone's life is in danger. Dismissed."

I pocketed the weapon, saluted, rotated on my heel as I had just been taught two weeks before, and left RVIPF headquarters.

I had done as commanded, locking the Webley in the safe, where it had remained ever since, with only its box of shells for company. I had never fired the gun. I had never made an arrest. I had never investigated a crime, or made a call to headquarters, until the call that brought the deputy commissioner to the government dock that day.

My quarterly reports to DC Lane had been the same bland paragraph for twenty years. No crimes, no incidents, no disruptions on Anegada, "that otherwise wild place." The volunteer fire brigade had a much more exciting life, watching a shack burn down or evacuating a child with appendicitis once every year or two. Virgin Islands Search and Rescue made a regular business of saving sailboaters who piled up on Horseshoe Reef. But crime, criminals, and the police work they generate were unknown to Anegada, until De White Rasta made his report of the dead man at Spanish Camp.

The British Virgin Islands as a whole experience a murder once or twice a decade. Most BVI homicides occur on Tortola, the rare result of a burst of anger in a not-very-angry place. As for the outer islands, only Virgin Gorda had had a killing in recent memory, a love-triangle murder solved in the first hour by the perpetrator's simultaneous report of the crime and confession.

Anegada's most recent murder had taken place in 1681. After a raid on a merchant vessel bound from Barbados to London, the pirate Bone had returned to his home at Bones Bight Pond on the north coast with two hostages. Captain Bone killed the hostages when the man-of-war sent to hunt him down appeared off Bones Bight, and attempted to hide the bodies by sinking them in Flamingo Pond. The high salinity of the pond brought the bodies back to the surface just as a squad from the Duke of York and Albany's Maritime Regiment of Foot on the hunt for Bone passed by. Bone was arrested and hanged at Barbados, as much for the piracy as for the murders. In the three centuries since, the crime that reaches back to Cain and Abel had not recurred on Anegada. It was, therefore, not unexpected that a report of a homicide would receive the personal attention of the second-ranking officer of the RVIPF.

Returning my salute, the deputy commissioner aimed a look of disdain at my uniform shirt, taking in the crusty sweat stains at the armpits and the blood and bits of brain on the sleeve. The air grew frostier as his eyes worked their way down to my nonregulation shorts and sandals.

I was saved from a dressing-down by the debarking of Rollie Stoutt, an inspector with the Scenes of Crime Unit of the Criminal Investigations Department, from the *St. Ursula*.

Or should I say, he is the Scenes of Crime Unit, as he is the only police officer in the unit. Overweight and soft as a freshly fluffed pillow, he hovered momentarily on the boat's gunwale before plunging onto the dock. An explosion of Bay Rum cologne traveled ashore with him. He slipped on some discarded fish entrails and nearly dropped the two aluminum equipment cases he carried.

DC Lane redirected his silent exasperation to Rollie for a moment and then turned back to me. You could almost hear the voice inside his head screaming that he was surrounded by incompetents but he bit back his anger and focused on the task at hand. "Let's get to your crime scene, Special Constable. You can fill us in on the way."

The DC strode the mile of sand to Spanish Camp with his shoes and socks on. Inspector Stoutt followed, wheezing asthmatically in the heat. His uniform pants were rolled to the knee and he carried his shoes, laces tied together, across his shoulder. Halfway to the crime scene, it became clear this was as far as he had ever walked without a rest break in his life.

On the drive and the walk to Spanish Camp, I told the DC and Inspector Stoutt the basic facts surrounding the crime, struggling for the right moment to disclose that it had been necessary to move the victim's body. That moment never did come. I decided to let circumstances speak for themselves after we arrived at the scene.

As we walked down the landward side of the dune at Spanish Camp, the crabs seemed mobilized to demonstrate the wisdom of my actions in moving the body. Drawn by the baking-flesh odor, they had returned, moving in zombie waves against the walls of the backpacker tent containing Professor Kelliher's remains.

Inspector Stoutt stretched yellow plastic POLICE LINE—DO NOT CROSS tape from sage bush to rock to cactus around the crime scene while the DC and I kicked crabs away from the tent. I had unzipped the tent fly and was about to pull the body feet first from the tent when Rollie placed his stubby fingers on my arm to stop me. He insisted on inspecting and photographing the body in place. He gamely squeezed through the tent flap with his Nikon, only to emerge a few seconds later. If ever a black man looked wan, it was Rollie. Even his accompanying cloud of cologne was inadequate protection from the rancid stench inside the tent. He asked us to pull the body out while he photographed the process.

There was no neat way to lift the professor's remains from the one-man tent, so DC Lane and I snapped on the white rubber gloves Rollie gave us and each took a leg. Rollie spread a plastic sheet at the tent's mouth and we tugged. The long afternoon in the greenhouselike interior of the tent had done the body no good but at least a leg did not come off in my hand.

The deputy commissioner was composed and businesslike. He leaned in to inspect the body without further touching it. Rollie, on the other hand, was as tentative as a schoolgirl doing her first dissection in biology class.

"Inspector, get a grip and get going or we'll be doing this in the dark," the DC barked.

Rollie bustled into action, snapping open his second aluminum equipment case. He pulled out a small tape recorder, placed it in my hand, and said, “Hold it near my mouth. It’s voice activated. I’m going to take photos and record a description of them as I go.”

The Nikon clicked and whirred. Rollie murmured a short summary after each shot.

“Photo one—full-body photo of white male victim. Appears to be late sixties to early seventies in age. Height five feet ten inches. Weight thirteen stone. Time of death unknown. Some bloating. Full rigor mortis has set in.

“Photo two—head of victim, full face on. Bullet entry wound in the forehead, above and slightly left of the bridge of the nose. It appears the bullet angled upward. The left eye is gone, probably due to the actions of scavengers postmortem. Flesh has also been eaten from parts of the nose and cheeks by postmortem scavengers.

“Photo three—close-up of the bullet entry wound.

“Photo four—top of skull, showing exit-wound area, and loss of significant portions of cranial bones and brain matter, probably caused by exiting bullet fragments. No bullet fragments apparent.

“Photo five—right side of head, showing remains of the right ear. Missing portions of the ear were probably removed by scavengers.

“Photo six—left side of head, with damage to the left ear, same cause as prior photo.

“Photo seven—torso. No apparent antemortem trauma.

Some flesh removed where not protected by clothing, again, probably postmortem action of scavengers.

"Photo eight—left hand, two fingers completely removed at base, remaining fingers with most skin and significant portions of flesh removed, again probably scavengers.

"Photo nine—right hand. Two fingers and thumb removed, including bone, to base of each digit. Remaining fingers show significant skin and flesh removed due to probable scavenger action postmortem."

Rollie paused, lowered the camera, and mopped sweat from his forehead and out of his eyes. The DC had been watching but now drifted over to inspect one of the excavations. Rollie directed his camera away from the body.

"Photo ten—entrance to tent from which remains were removed. To the right of the entrance appear to be discharged stomach contents or vomit, source unknown."

"That was me," I interrupted. Now, with the DC a safe distance away, seemed the best time to raise the topic of moving the body. "It happened after I moved the body inside the tent."

The camera descended from Rollie's eyes. "You moved the body?"

"It was the only way to keep the crabs and gulls from eating it up while I went back to get help." My explanation had no effect on the look of incredulity on Rollie's face.

The DC had meandered back within earshot in time to catch Rollie's follow-up question to my confession. "You moved the body from where?" He pronounced the words with slow, cold precision.

I showed the DC and Rollie where I had found the body. Rollie continued snapping photographs, shooting the route I had taken with Professor Kelliher's body in reverse from the tent to the original location, focusing on a drag mark in the sand here, a bit of brain there.

When we got to where the body had originally lain, Rollie photographed the remains of my breakfast in the sand. "You again?" he asked.

I nodded.

The DC muttered unintelligibly under his breath, brought himself up to his full stature, and ordered me to go for some assistance to help bring the remains back to The Settlement.

The sun was only an hour from the horizon when I returned with four of the men from the volunteer fire brigade. They carried a canvas stretcher between them. DC Lane met us at the POLICE LINE tape and forbade me from stepping inside its perimeter.

I stood and watched, alone, from the top of the sandbank as they rolled Professor Kelliher's corpse onto the stretcher to begin its journey home.

Chapter Five

At a few minutes before midnight, Deputy Commissioner Lane sat in my chair behind the metal desk in the one-room Anegada police station. The contents of Paul Kelliher's pockets and the small backpack found in his tent were in two orderly rows on my blotter, just as the DC had unpacked them. The professor had traveled light, with the only identification documents in his effects being his passport and a Massachusetts driver's license. There was also a Visa card, seventy-three US dollars in cash, and a cell phone with no numbers stored in its contacts and only calls to the American Airlines flight reservations number in its call log. All the clothing consisted of the Anegada uniform of T-shirts, shorts, and underwear. The toiletries were basic as well—a razor, shaving soap, toothbrush, toothpaste, and deodorant.

"You are no longer involved in this investigation, Special Constable Creque," DC Lane intoned in his best James

Earl Jones voice. "Your failure to preserve the crime scene—no, your purposeful disturbance of the scene—was contrary to RVIPF procedures and may have endangered this investigation. Perhaps that is the way you do things here on Anegada but that is not the way we conduct ourselves as members of the Royal Virgin Islands Police Force. You are suspended for two weeks without pay, and instructed to take a remedial seminar on crime scene preservation online at headquarters in Road Town after you have served your suspension. Fortunately for you, and unfortunately for the RVIPF, I do not have a spare police officer to send to Anegada and it seems we need a police presence here more than any time in the last twenty years. Your suspension will be served at such later time as I designate."

The DC went on. "For now, copy down Professor Kelliher's driver's license and passport information. Then locate and inform his next of kin of his death. Put them in contact with the coroner's office so they can claim the body when the autopsy is completed. That is all, Special Constable." He passed the two documents across the desk to me. I took them, saluted, and left with the realization that my professional life was going almost as well as my personal life.

The next morning I was back at my desk in the police station by seven a.m. Deputy Commissioner Lane, Inspector Stoutt, and Professor Kelliher's body had departed on the *St. Ursula* at dawn, the body in a machinery crate lined with garbage bags and packed in ice from the meat locker at the Reef Hotel.

There was no doubt that a sitting of the coroner's inquest in Road Town, held in all cases of unexpected death, would reach a verdict of homicide. A man had been killed, apparently with a firearm, on the island that is my home. As the only police presence, I felt a strong need to find the killer or killers and bring them to justice. But DC Lane had been explicit and so I turned to the task assigned to me.

I thought it would be easy to locate Paul Kelliher's next of kin using his passport and driver's license information. I began with the passport information because I thought it should be reliable and because often an emergency contact can be obtained using it. Besides, my second cousin Sheila Creque works in the San Juan, Puerto Rico, office of US Immigration and Customs Enforcement.

I called her on the landline and she was able to confirm the information on Professor Kelliher's passport. After speaking with her supervisor, she faxed a form to the administrator's office to be completed to obtain the emergency contact information. Ten minutes after faxing back the completed form, I had Paul Kelliher's emergency contact: Bonnie Kelliher, wife, 52 Fisher Avenue, Roxbury Crossing, Boston, Massachusetts, telephone 617-754-5966. The address matched the one on the professor's driver's license.

I had never delivered news like this before, so I took a minute to compose myself and think about what I would say. Be gentle, be factual, and express condolences, I told myself. I had seen it on TV. I dialed the Boston number.

"Patriot Pizza and Spuckies, can I take ya ordah?"

Derailed from my rehearsed lines, I took a moment before I spoke. "I am trying to reach Bonnie Kelliher," I stammered.

"Who?" The girl's Boston accent was as thick as clam chowder, her tone brusque.

"B-O-N-N-I-E K-E-L-L-I-H-E-R," I spelled.

"Nobody here by that name. This is a pizza parlor. Ya wanna order a pizza or not?"

"This is important. I am a police constable in the British Virgin Islands—"

"Yeah, an' I'm the friggin' queen of England." The line clicked dead.

I checked the phone to make certain I had dialed the correct number. It matched the number on the fax from US ICE. Thinking the emergency contact number might have been a typo, I went to the administrator's office and sat down at the computer terminal. Pamela Pickering's Acer PC and its grimy keyboard were the sole link between the Internet and the government of the BVI on Anegada. A search of the Boston white pages revealed several Kellihers but no Paul or Bonnie. No P. Kelliher or B. Kelliher. No number was listed for 52 Fisher Avenue. Maybe the number was unlisted. Not unusual. I could see where a man who spent as much time alone as Paul Kelliher might value his privacy.

Knowing that Professor Kelliher was a member of the Boston University biology faculty, I located the BU biology department home page and called the number listed there.

"Angela Petto, assistant to the chair, how may I help you?" The clam chowder accent again, though thinner and more courteous this time. A mental image of a plumpish Ms. Petto, wearing out-of-style eyeglasses and a pilling pink sweater, conjured itself in my head for no reason.

I explained who I was, that I was sorry to inform her that Professor Paul Kelliher had been killed during his research trip to Anegada, and that I hoped she could provide correct contact information for his next of kin.

"Who is Professor Paul Kelliher?" Ms. Petto asked.

"He is a member of the faculty of your biology department. He has been coming to Anegada in the British Virgin Islands for the past five years to do research on an endangered species here."

"Honey, I've been heah for nineteen yeahs, the last ten as assistant to the department chair, and I nevah heard of any Professor Kelliher. And as of right now, none of our faculty members are conducting field research in the Caribbean, the British Virgin Islands, or any place called Anegada." She pronounced it "Ann-ah-gay-der."

Ms. Petto tried to be helpful. "Maybe you have the wrong department. Let me check the university directory." The clicking of the keyboard in Boston was as clear as if it were on the desk in front of me. "No, Constable. There is no Paul Kelliher listed as an employee of the university or as a student. Sorry."

"That's all right. Thank you for your help."

She hung up.

I decided to go the police route with my problem. A couple of faxes on RVIPF letterhead, followed by a phone call switched from one division of the Boston Police Department to another, and then another, ended with my speaking to Detective Sergeant Brett Donovan in the Missing Persons Unit.

Unlike everyone else I had spoken to in Boston, Detective Sergeant Donovan had a bland Midwestern accent and time on his hands. I explained my difficulties and he quickly tried to locate Professor Kelliher in his BPD database. Nothing. He accessed the Massachusetts Registry of Motor Vehicles and turned up the same driver's license information I had and nothing more. Undaunted, he volunteered to drive to the Fisher Avenue address. "I should be back in an hour," he said.

I called back in precisely one hour.

"Missing Persons. Detective Sergeant Donovan," he answered.

"Special Constable Creque from the Virgin Islands calling to follow up."

"Yeah, Constable, I checked out your Number Fifty-Two Fisher Avenue. It was a wild goose chase. There is no Number Fifty-Two. There is a Fifty-Four Fisher Avenue and a Fifty, but where Fifty-Two should be is just a vacant lot with some trees on it behind the baseball field at McLaughlin Playground. I knocked on the door at Number Fifty and the resident there never heard of Paul or Bonnie Kelliher. The guy in Fifty had lived there for ten years. Looks like a bad address on the driver's license and passport. Maybe your decedent did not want to be found."

"I'm beginning to think that, Detective Sergeant. Do you

have any ideas about what else I might do to locate his next of kin?"

"If you get me a set of prints I could run it through our system and see if that turns up anything. And a DNA sample might work if he had previously been tested, although I would need clearance from my boss to run that."

"The remains are at the coroner's office on another island right now, so I can't provide prints to you at this moment," I said.

"No problem. Call me if you want to run the prints or if you need anything else run down on this end. Good luck, Constable."

"Thank you for your efforts, Detective Sergeant."

The seemingly simple task DC Lane had assigned to me had certainly become more complicated. Find the next of kin of a dead man, whose supposed employer has no record of him, with an address that does not exist. I decided to try one more avenue before calling the deputy commissioner to admit failure.

Chapter Six

Cobbled together from plywood, driftwood, rope, and corrugated tin, the Cow Wreck Beach Bar and Grill combined the attention to form of a Gaudí cathedral with the orderliness of a junkyard. Its only truly valuable assets were a beer cooler, a hot plate, and Belle Lloyd. The beer cooler was obvious in its utility. The hot plate was the genesis of the best conch fritters on Anegada and perhaps in the entire Caribbean. Belle Lloyd, bartender, cook, hostess, and sole proprietor, was the favorite aunt, best friend, and confidante of all who set foot on the bar's pale pink sand floor. Cow Wreck Bay was out of the way, even for Anegada, but Belle's warm smile and easy humor made the ramshackle bar a getaway place for native Anegadians and tourists alike.

The Cow Wreck Beach Bar and Grill was also the closest thing Paul Kelliher had to a base of operations on Anegada.

When the professor took a break from his field research expeditions, his destination was always the seaward of the four stools at Belle's unfinished plywood bar. If anyone would have information on him, it would be Belle.

I arrived at Cow Wreck in the early afternoon. Belle had just finished serving a lunch of goat stew to a couple at the bar. I had seen them around, middle-aged Americans staying at the Reef Hotel. They were the only ones in the place and whispered excitedly to each other about having stumbled onto this gem and having it all to themselves on a perfect day. Both Belle and I had seen this kind of excitement before; it happened every time a new traveler came to Belle's establishment.

"You want some lunch, Teddy? I got one serving of goat water left." Belle gestured toward the pot on the hot plate.

"I'd love it, Belle."

She ladled from the pot and placed a steaming plate in front of me. The aroma hit and I instantly salivated. I would crawl over broken glass for a plate of Belle's goat water. Anyone in their right mind would.

The day's lunch service completed, Belle sat on a high stool she kept behind the bar. "So what's with you, Teddy?"

"I'm here on police business today. Paul Kelliher is dead. De White Rasta found him over at Spanish Camp, shot in the head. I'm hoping you have some information to help me get in touch with his family in the States." As I said this, a look of shock and surprise appeared on Belle's face.

"He shot himself in the head?" Even as she said the words, it was clear she believed that was not something Professor Kelliher would do.

"No. No gun was found. Someone shot him and I don't know who or why," I said. "Do you know anything about his family?"

"I know he had a wife. Bonnie, I think he said, but he never talked much about her, only mentioned her name. He said she never came on his trips because she didn't like the heat and camping out 'in the field,' as he called it. He never mentioned any children or parents. He never talked very much about personal stuff. He was all about the rock iguana, and had anybody looked in this or that part of the east side for them. He was always asking if anyone was doing any poking around over there. He said he didn't want to see the habitat of the lizards destroyed. Wanted to make sure no one was disturbing them or going over there killing them to eat like we did in the old days. That was usually the extent of the conversation until he'd had enough rum smoothies that he had to sleep it off."

"Where did he do that?"

"I keep a cot in back. He kept some of his stuff here, too. Come on, I'll show you." Belle led me around the open end of the back wall of the bar to a lean-to storage room on the other side. Behind the cases of beer, propane canisters, and other detritus of the bar business was a folding camp cot. At the foot of the cot were two molded plastic storage containers, stacked one atop the other.

"His stuff is in those two containers," Belle said, pointing.

I opened the top container. It must have served as Kelliher's wardrobe, as it contained several pairs of shorts, a half dozen T-shirts, khaki pants, and one long-sleeved shirt.

The second container held a spiral notebook, like the kind schoolchildren use. I opened it and saw that the first dozen pages were filled with writing, an incoherent mix of letters and numbers. I thought it might be some kind of code. There was no discernible system or pattern to the letters and numbers, so I put it aside to revisit later.

Below the notebook were several folded maps. The first was a 1977 map of Anegada prepared by the British Ministry of Overseas Development. I had seen prints of this map many times before. It was the only quality modern map of Anegada and copies were for sale at the Reef Hotel and several places in Road Town on Tortola. The map had an arc drawn in pencil with the point of the radius in the area of Spanish Camp. Within the arc was a scattering of X marks, also in pencil, with no notations or explanation.

Under the 1977 survey map was a photocopy of a map entitled “Anegada with Its Reefs” by R. H. Schomburgk, dated 1832. Unlike the survey map, Schomburgk’s map actually contained the designation “Spanish Camp” on Anegada’s east side. The words were double underlined in pencil, the only notation on the photocopy.

A manila envelope was folded beneath the two maps. Inside was a crude drawing done on a single legal-size sheet, crisp-dry with age. A heavy pencil line bisected the page lengthwise, with the word “pond” inside an irregular circle left of the line, and an X between the line and the circle. If it was intended as a map, it left much to be desired.

At the bottom of the container, I found a SOG-TAC

push-button knife with a matte black blade, and a rectangular tube that looked like a small flashlight with no bulb. There was a switch labeled “on/off” at the base of the tube and a cap at the opposite end. Opening the cap revealed two metal prongs or posts a quarter inch long. I pushed the switch and a blue bolt of electricity crackled between the posts. Belle jumped back and let out a short yelp. I released the switch. The smell of ozone hung in the close quarters of the lean-to. The tube seemed to be some type of electroshock weapon, not the sort of equipment a biologist brings to the field. The knife was not exactly a camp knife either, its wicked blade and matte finish making it something I would expect a commando, not a scientist, to carry.

“Did he ever show you any of this?” I asked Belle.

“No. What is that electrical thing?” Belle focused on the tube like it was a poisonous snake in the room.

“I don’t know, Belle.” There was obviously much I did not know and the trip to Cow Wreck only raised more questions without providing any answers.

Thanking Belle, I put the two containers of Kelliher’s belongings in the Land Rover and headed back to The Settlement.

I looked forward to telling the deputy commissioner that I had failed to find Paul Kelliher’s next of kin with the eagerness of a penitent headed to confession after a debauched weekend capped by a mortal sin. Circumstances spared me. When I called headquarters in Road Town, DC Lane and the commissioner were in a meeting with the premier and Her

Majesty's governor, presumably to report on the murder and develop the best spin to prevent an exodus of tourists and their dollars. Consuela Lettsome, the DC's secretary since forever, transferred me to Inspector Stoutt.

Rollie listened with polite disinterest as I described my efforts and then unhelpfully suggested that I keep trying. I asked if he wanted me to send Kelliher's personal effects over on the next ferry.

"Keep them there. I don't have a lot of room in the evidence lockup, and they are not really evidence, anyway." Rollie was as incurious as a stenographer.

My shift as special constable was over and my shift at the power generator would begin in two hours. I had left a note for Icilda that I would be home for dinner, so I turned the Land Rover in that direction.

"Betty Wheatley told me that Professor Kelliher was killed out at Spanish Camp," Icilda said to greet me as I came through the door. We had not spoken since before the body was found, between her late dinner shift at the Reef Hotel and my departure before she awoke that morning. Not that there was anything unusual about that. In the last few years, we had gone days at a time without seeing or speaking to each other due to the overlapping shifts of our various jobs. "Was it some kind of accident?"

"He was shot." I flopped into my chair at the kitchen table.

"Shot? Who would want to do that to him? He doesn't

have an enemy on Anegada." She placed a glass of iced tea before me. A cool bead of condensation from the glass dripped into my lap as I drank.

"He must have at least one enemy, here or somewhere. Someone felt the need to shoot him in the middle of the forehead."

"Dear Jesus have mercy on that man's eternal soul." Churchy Icilda. She never missed a chance to put what she heard on Sunday morning to use during the rest of the week. "Do you have a suspect?"

"I don't have anything. I am not on the case." I went on to recount my transgressions at the crime scene and DC Lane's removal of me from the investigation. Icilda took it in with the same aplomb she displayed when Kevin failed to pick up his clothes from his bedroom floor. Maybe she just didn't care.

There had been a time when she had cared but that time was long ago now. There had been a time when I had cared, too, cared about Icilda Faulkner and everything she said and did. I guess you could say we thought we were in love, once, when life was new and we were young. We had seemed to ourselves and others to be a good match, the two most ambitious and lively offspring of two old Anegada families.

So we got married and for a time the life we had hoped to make together appeared to be ours. Then Kevin and Tamia came along, and multiple jobs, and there was always a boat to repair, or housework to be done, and now we just went through the motions. At least what Icilda did seemed like she was just going through the motions. The girl I had thought I loved, and who I thought had loved me, the young wife who had told me her dreams, had not had much to say to me these last few years that didn't pertain to the business of the day, the logistics of feeding and transporting kids, or the schedule of church services for the week. And, shame on me, I let it happen, drifted like some tired old barge along with the current, until I was lost, resigned and just going through the motions, too. Maybe the point had been reached where I just didn't care, either.

"My only assignment now is to find and notify his next of kin," I said. Icilda merely grunted as she spooned peas and rice and some fried yellowtail onto a plate for me. Kevin and Tamia came rattling in from outside, in a typical brother-sister dispute over some slight, real or imagined, that they demanded I mediate. It was clear that the discussion of Paul Kelliher's demise and my duties related to it was over.

Chapter Seven

Instead of the usual nap, that night's shift at the electric plant provided a chance to reflect on the events of the last forty-eight hours. A man was dead on Anegada. His killer might still be here or could be a thousand miles away by now. I had altered the crime scene and impeded or maybe even ruined the investigation. The murder weapon was a gun, and there were no guns on the island, other than the Webley locked in the police station safe and a rusty shotgun or two in The Settlement, left over from the days of flamingo hunting. There was no readily apparent motive for the murder. The victim was not the man he portrayed himself to be. The victim's possessions included maps, drawings, writings in code, and weapons, all items he did not need to conduct the research he'd led everyone on Anegada to believe he had been doing for the last several years.

My musings were interrupted by a cough from the number two diesel generator, followed by a mechanical sigh and the generator's complete shutdown. The Anegada power grid was now overloaded, with the older number one generator unable to keep up with the early evening demand for electricity. If I did not cut power to part of the island, the grid would fail completely and all of Anegada would black out.

I made the choice I had made a hundred times before, cutting off electricity to The Settlement and keeping power flowing to the western half of the island. The unwritten rule was to never kill the lights at the Reef Hotel, Neptune's Treasure, the Pomato Point Restaurant, and the Lobster Trap grill when the tourists were having their sundowners and the restaurant kitchens were in the midst of preparing their evening meals. A little hardship for the locals was preferable to any discomfort for the tourists and their credit cards. It was always the choice made; any disruption of the relaxation of the bareboaters, honeymooners, and bonefish anglers equated to an interruption of cash flow for Anegada and the British Virgin Islands.

An hour passed as I disassembled and cleaned the number two generator's fuel filter, hoping this simple fix would do the trick. I tried a restart. Sputtering and gasping like a rescued drowning victim, the generator finally jolted back to life.

The lights came on in The Settlement and at that moment I knew in the pit of my stomach that the murder would never be solved by Rollie Stoutt. It would never be solved because Paul Kelliher, or whoever he was, was not a tourist, or a local belonger, and thus he did not matter. It would never be solved because that would mean telling the world that the pristine beaches and the laid-back bars and restaurants of Anegada are located in a place where a drug deal can go bad, a robbery can end in death, or a jealous lover can bring in a gun to exact revenge. It would never be solved because a solution would expose something dark, sinister, and ugly about a place that is a Caribbean fantasy of tranquillity and leisure. The absence of a solution meant the eventual return of the serenity and calm without the blemish that the hard facts would cause. The inconvenience of the murder would simply fade away.

I knew it was not intentional. It was the product of our collective subconscious. Rollie Stoutt would work away at the investigation, but not too hard and not in a way that would dirty his hands by digging deep into troublesome facts. Rollie would periodically report his lack of progress to Deputy Commissioner Lane, who would report to the commissioner, who would report to the premier, until the item fell away from each of their meeting agendas. With no family demanding answers and calling for justice, whoever had committed the murder at Spanish Camp would remain at liberty and unknown.

And just as I knew this murder would never be solved by Inspector Stoutt, I knew I had to try to solve it. Maybe I needed to try to satisfy myself that Anegada was still a simple, peaceful, crime-free place. Maybe I needed to see the person who had left Kelliher to the crabs and gulls answer for what he had done. Maybe I felt the need to redeem myself with the deputy commissioner. Maybe I was in the middle years of a life of too many uneventful patrols around the island, too many dull shifts at the power plant, and too many sunny days with no good news and no bad news melting one into another. But I knew I had to try. I would start the next morning.

As I walked home from work at eight, I got a hug and kiss from Kevin and Tamia, who were on their way to school along with the three dozen other children who attended the Anegada School. Icilda was working the breakfast and lunch shift at the Reef Hotel and was already gone when I arrived. After a breakfast of johnnycake and tepid coffee from the morning's pot, I changed into my uniform pants and shirt. If I was going to conduct a police investigation, I would look the part.

There had not been much sleep for me at the power plant. The hum of the diesel generators had provided bland background music as I ruminated over the scant information I had about Paul Kelliher and his death. One thing was certain: he was not studying iguanas. There was not one indication in his belongings that he was doing any biology fieldwork—no photographs, no field notes, no books on iguanas or biology. He *was* doing something that had him, and maybe the person who killed him, digging holes all over Spanish Camp. And keeping coded notes. And carrying weapons and maps with Xs on them. It had to be treasure hunting.

Paul Kelliher was certainly not the first to arrive on Anegada in search of buried treasure. Every year or two a single hunter or a group would arrive, hurrying off the *Bomba Charger*, the fast ferry from Road Town, with metal detectors, shovels, maps, and unwarranted optimism. After a week of digging in the sun and heat, they would make the return ferry trip, exhausted, sunburned, and disappointed. Several pirates, including Captain Bone and Black Sam Bellamy, were said to have buried Spanish gold and silver inland from the north shore beaches, so the quest for treasure was not entirely misplaced. If Paul Kelliher had been onto something involving treasure, there was one man on Anegada who might have an idea what that something was, so that was where I decided to begin.

Wendell George was one of the few residents of Anegada who was not born here. Wendell, an Antiguan, had set up a restaurant on the far western side of the island at Pomato Point when I was still a small child, bringing a mistress, and a penchant for privacy, with him. He presumably chose the isolation of Anegada and Pomato Point to make it difficult for his wife to chase him down.

It must have worked because no wife ever appeared. Wendell's willowy mistress, whose name nobody knew and whom everyone privately called "the Mistress," cooked wondrous meals of conch stew, pumpkin soup, fungee, and ducana for him and the very occasional patrons of the Pomato Point Restaurant. She never spoke to anyone but Wendell, never went to The Settlement, and always wore a pensive smile. For his part in the business, Wendell took food orders, ran the cash register, and otherwise dealt with the public with the disapproving demeanor of a Catholic school nun reprimanding an unruly child.

Wendell also hunted treasure. One of the rooms of the Pomato Point Restaurant was what he called his museum, a collection of bottles, small coins, grapeshot, broken plates, and buttons he had found while searching the island for Bone's and Bellamy's plunder. The museum was supposed to be a tourist draw for the restaurant, but the place was so out of the way it was empty most nights. Still, Wendell appeared to prosper, dressing well and importing a new Toyota Land Cruiser from San Juan every other year. Speculation in The Settlement was that not all of Wendell's finds made their way to his museum, with the best being disposed of on yearly trips he took to Miami.

The Mistress was sweeping sand from the green and black glazed tiles of the stoop when I drove into the sandpit that passed for a parking lot at the Pomato Point Restaurant. She smiled warmly at me and disappeared inside before I could get out of the Land Rover. A dour Wendell emerged a second later, blinking in the white morning sun. My greeting to him was acknowledged only with a nod. I decided to break the ice with the "T" word.

"Wendell, I have come to talk with you about treasure."

Wendell's entire body stiffened. Perspiration beaded on his forehead and above his pencil-thin mustache. His eyes betrayed a disturbingly sexual mix of greed and pleasure to their innermost depth. Then, after a moment, he regained his composure and resumed his poker face.

"What about treasure?" He was as coy as a pawnbroker.

"I take it you heard about the man killed at Spanish Camp."

"I've heard. It's all over the island. The iguana professor. What does that have to do with treasure?" Wendell focused like a laser on the important topic, dead man be damned.

"I think he was hunting treasure. I think that may have something to do with his death," I said.

"What makes you think he was hunting treasure?" God forbid we get off topic.

"His tent had a good number of excavations around it. All waist deep, and all left open after they were dug, like he didn't find what he was digging for and was in a hurry to move on to the next place. Judging by the number of holes, he had to have been digging for a month or two at least."

"Just because a man digs holes doesn't mean he's digging for treasure. Maybe it was something to do with his iguana research." Wendell pretended to play devil's advocate, but he sensed there was more. He was barely able to contain himself.

This was so easy, it was almost fun. I cast the bait. "He also had some marked-up maps, a drawing, and a notebook that seems to be written in code."

Wendell smiled, a grudging, closed-lipped smile that showed no teeth and might have been mistaken for a sneer on a happier individual. It was the first time I had ever seen him smile. Maybe it was the first time he had ever smiled. "I could take a look at those if you want some help," he offered.

I went to the Land Rover and brought out the maps,

drawing, and notebook. We moved to a table in the cool interior of the restaurant. Wendell crooked a finger in the general direction of the kitchen. A minute later, the Mistress materialized with a tray holding two glasses and an iced pitcher of guava juice. She disappeared before I could get out a thank-you.

Wendell spread the two maps and the legal-sheet drawing on the table, weighting the edges of the maps with silverware. He pondered them for a few seconds before he spoke.

"Well, we've both seen the '77 survey map a hundred times, but I don't have a clue about the pencil markings on it. I have seen copies of the Schomburgk map, and I saw the original at the Royal Geographical Society five years ago when I visited London. It took some persuasion to get a look at it but the original told me nothing that a decent photocopy could not. As far as I know, it is the only map showing Spanish Camp, even though everyone on Anegada seems to know where it is."

Wendell placed a stubby finger on the drawing. "This drawing looks like the pond and shoreline by Spanish Camp, but it also could be a rough sketch of the area between the beach and any of the ponds on Anegada. No way to tell from the thing. There is just not enough detail, no landmarks, no compass rose, and no map key or writings, other than the word 'pond.' You know it's not very old, just from the paper.

"Is the drawing, or the drawing together with the maps, a treasure map?" Wendell stated the question for himself. "Hell, I've been to libraries and archives in London, Amsterdam, Lisbon, and Madrid, poring over their contents for days, and none of them contained an honest-to-goodness treasure map. If you hid treasure, why make a map that might fall into someone else's hands and allow them to find it? Just remember the landmarks and don't tell anyone. There is no such thing as a treasure map."

Wendell paused and leaned in to me conspiratorially. "Besides, I've been all over Spanish Camp with a metal detector. There is nothing to find there. No one ever stayed there, not Columbus and not any pirate. There is no harbor and no protection from storm swell. Bones Bight and Windlass Bight are where any treasure should be on Anegada. That's the area where Bone and Bellamy had their hideouts. You don't need me to tell you that."

Wendell shifted his attention. "Can I have a look at that notebook?"

I passed the notebook to him. He flipped through every page of it, slowly. After half an hour, he leaned back and said, "I haven't a clue what it means. It certainly seems to be written in a code, probably not difficult to break but not like what I have seen when it comes to codes from the buccaneer days. The old Spanish and Portuguese coded navigational logs I reviewed in archives were extremely simple by modern standards. Usually there was a key or codebook that matched a random letter, number, or symbol to the actual letter intended. You decoded by having the code key.

"What you have here doesn't seem to be a simple keyed code because of the frequency of the more common letters, like 'e,' 't,' and 'a.' If it were a keyed code, the frequency of the letters *substituted* for 'e,' 't' and 'a' would be greater than that of 'e,' 't,' or 'a.' That isn't the case. It might be some other type of substitution code that is still fairly simple, but with no key needed to decode a message. A classic form is a Caesar shift, where you replace one letter with another a fixed number of places away in the alphabet. For example, shift each letter by three and 'C-A-T' becomes 'F-D-W' in code. Caesar shifts were used as far back as the Roman Empire. Play with a Caesar shift long enough and you will eventually work it out. But most likely it is a rail fence."

"A rail fence?" I asked.

"Yes. Take the words you want to encode and write every other letter one line down. 'RAIL FENCE' becomes . . ." Wendell pulled a pen from his pocket and jotted on a paper napkin:

RIFNE

ALEC

"Then recombine along the rows and your code message is RIFNE+ALEC=RIFNEALEC. A rail fence code in its most basic form is very easily broken, but it can be combined with dead rows of letters and numbers between the rows formed by the real message to make it more difficult. Add a row of random letters and numbers to the 'RAIL FENCE' message like so:"

RIFNE

7QN3Z

ALEC

"Then it becomes RIFNE+7QN3Z+ALEC=RIFNE7QN3ZALEC. If you do not know the number of letters and numbers in each dead row and the number of dead rows in the message, it can be quite difficult to decipher without a computer program designed for code breaking. The good news about this code is that it is all letters and numbers, with no symbols. That should make breaking it a little easier."

"How easy is easier?" I asked. I was fast altering my definition of "easy." It used to be as easy as pie; as easy as falling off a log; as easy as shooting fish in a barrel. Now "easy" meant grinding away deciphering pages of seemingly random letters and numbers for who knows how long.

"Probably weeks if you had code-breaking experience and devoted full time to it." Wendell's enthusiasm over access to the notebook visibly waned as he said the words. The magnitude of the task hit home for me when he did not even volunteer to attempt it.

The Mistress returned, clearing the table with downcast eyes. I gathered the maps, drawing, and notebook. "Thanks, Wendell. You have been of great assistance."

The light of greed dimming in his eyes, Wendell shrugged.

Chapter Eight

The first mile of the road from Pomato Point to The Settlement sets the island standard for disrepair. As I crawled the Land Rover along from pothole to pothole, I mulled over what I had learned from Wendell.

The two maps were of little help. The drawing was crude and generic. The key to what Paul Kelliher was doing at Spanish Camp, if there was a key, lay in the coded text of the notebook. The code had to be broken.

There was a chance of accomplishing this myself, I supposed, but I had no code-breaking experience and, as far as I knew, no particular flair for such a task. Sending the notebook to RVIPF headquarters with my recommendation for decoding would guarantee its relegation to the immobile heap I was sure existed on Rollie Stoutt's desk. Asking Pamela Pickering for help would devolve into a dispute about who had authority over whom. Besides, she was such a vacant cow that the task would never be completed if she deigned to take it on.

At the roundabout near Setting Point, the weirdly logical solution to my need for code-breaking assistance manifested itself in the form of Anthony Wedderburn. De Rasta was smoking a comically large fatty of shag as he strolled in the direction of The Settlement. I pulled over to offer a ride and he climbed into the passenger seat, enveloped in an acrid cloud of homegrown-tobacco smoke.

"Good day, Teddy. Would you care for a hit?" Anthony said, extending the business end of the fatty toward me. "This is my best crop in a couple of years. Once I get it properly dried and aged, it will rival the finest our Cuban neighbors have to offer."

De Rasta grew his shag in a small patch near Saltheap Point, watering the yellow-leafed plants with rainwater caught in a limestone sinkhole. I once made the mistake of trying a puff of his homegrown. The taste was somewhere between compost and wet-dog-on-fire. On this day, I respectfully declined.

Anthony slouched back against the seat, took a big drag, and peered at me through bloodshot eyes.

"If it is not too presumptuous, old man, you look as though you carry the weight of the world on your shoulders." De Rasta's tone was one of genuine concern.

"It's Professor Kelliher's murder, Anthony. Everywhere I turn I find more questions than answers. I can't even manage to locate his next of kin." I gave a brief description of my failures to date, ending with the morning's visit to Wendell George and the coded notebook. De Rasta either nodded sympathetically or was bouncing from the washboard road. I couldn't tell which.

"I can help you with the notebook," De Rasta said cheerfully. "Back in my other life I was a bit of a lonely boy, and I used to play with codes and such. Some said I had a knack for it, especially codes based on words. I used to do the *Times* jumbo every day in ink, timed with a stopwatch. My best time was twenty-seven minutes, forty-two seconds. That is less than sixteen seconds per clue, if that is of interest to you."

The voice inside me questioned whether it was prudent to turn my best clue to Professor Kelliher's identity over to this perpetually buzzed member of the aristocracy. After a brief hesitation, I decided to do it. There really were no other viable alternatives, and after all, his family had ruled the mother country for a millennium or more. That alone spoke volumes about their native intelligence and capacity for intrigue.

"You're hired," I said, "but the pay's a bit thin."

"Not a problem, Teddy. My unpretentious standard of living permits me to undertake the task for only modest compensation."

" 'Thin' as in 'no pay.' "

"Well, then, it looks as if we have a deal, old man."

When we reached The Settlement, I left De Rasta and the notebook in the midweek quiet of the Methodist church. Pastor Lloyd was not around and no one else would interrupt him there. He fairly danced through the front door in his eagerness to begin, the coded notebook in hand.

The events of the last few days had almost made me forget the dilemma I faced in my private life. I guess murder will do that to a man. A reminder of my ongoing personal drama came in the form of a radio call from Pamela Pickering advising that VI Birds was flying in a newlywed couple from St. Thomas for a stay at the Reef Hotel. I would be needed at the airport to pass them through customs.

A Jeep from the Reef Hotel, keys in the ignition, awaited the couple in the airport parking lot. A sultry-eyed Cat Wells walked the lovebirds through my cursory customs check, and I gave them directions to the hotel after stamping their passports.

"Watch out for cattle on the road," I called after them. They were pasty pale and only had eyes for each other. In two days they would be sunburned and quarreling their way to marital bliss.

Cat lingered in the terminal after the couple departed. "The days without you have been long and lonely, lover. I have three hours before I pick up my next charter in St. Thomas. I told the dispatcher I'd lay over here for an hour." She arched an eyebrow and ran her finger along my bicep. The touch was so electric I half expected to smell ozone. "I brought my suit. We could go to Windlass Bight for a swim."

We both knew that was not why we were going to Windlass Bight. She lay across the front seat of the Land Rover with her head in my lap as we drove to the beach. When we arrived, we tore the clothes from each other like animals, satisfying our hunger against a mimosa tree. Afterward, we did swim, though no suits were used.

The time for conversation arrived only when we had dressed and began the drive back to the airport. Cat leaned into my shoulder as I eased back onto the sand road.

"I heard a rumor that the call you got while I was here the other day actually was a dead man. A murder. Some tourist from the States," Cat said, speaking into my neck.

"Yes, the man was dead, murdered, but he was not a tourist. It was a fellow named Paul Kelliher. He held himself out to be a Boston University professor doing biology fieldwork on the rock iguana. He has been coming here for the last several winters. We all took him at his word, but when I started looking for his next of kin, there was no trace of him to be found. The address on his ID doesn't exist and no one at Boston University has ever heard of him. One thing is certain, though. Someone knew enough about him to want to shoot him."

"You don't think it was just a random incident, or a robbery?" Cat asked.

"Where he was, you had to work just to find him. If someone wanted to commit a robbery, there were plenty of easier victims. And there was a set of footprints seen that led from the parking area at Flash of Beauty right to where the crime took place. No, whoever did it knew exactly where he was and had a specific reason to go out there and kill him."

"What are you doing with the investigation?" Cat inquired with casual curiosity.

For the third time in two days I was forced to recite the tale of my shortcomings at the crime scene and my removal from the investigation. After a coo of sympathy, Cat asked who was heading the investigation.

"Rollie Stoutt, an inspector with the Scenes of Crime Unit, has the case as nearly as I can tell. His investigation so far consists of sitting in his office in Road Town waiting for the results of the autopsy. I can give the results of the autopsy right now. 'The decedent succumbed as the result of a single gunshot wound to the forehead, slightly above and to the left of the bridge of the nose. Massive brain trauma ensued, and death was instantaneous.' Rollie has not come back to Anegada to interview anyone, has not spoken to me except for a call I initiated when I couldn't locate the next of kin, and didn't even want to see the victim's personal effects from the Cow Wreck Beach Bar."

"He kept personal effects at Cow Wreck?" Cat nuzzled in as we bounced through the airport entrance.

"Just a few clothes, some maps, a sketch or drawing, and a notebook. The notebook is written in some kind of code."

"Code? Why would a biologist keep a notebook in code?"

"There wouldn't seem to be any reason, if he was a biologist, but it appears he was not," I said.

"Are you going to try to break the code?"

"I gave it to Anthony Wedderburn and he is working on it."

Cat suppressed a snorting half laugh. She had been around Anegada long enough to encounter Anthony as he stumbled about in a ganja-fogged stupor. “De White Rasta? That pot-addled vagrant? What can he possibly know about codes? And even if he does know something about them, he doesn’t stay straight long enough to string together a coherent sentence, let alone break a code. How did you pick him?”

“He said he could do it. And he’s the best choice I have.” It sounded hollow even as I said it.

Cat lifted her head from my shoulder as we pulled to a stop near the vacant airport terminal. She kissed me lightly on the lips and gave a single shake of her head. As she latched the door of the Land Rover and turned toward the helicopter on the tarmac, I heard the snort-laugh repeated.

When things are not going well, everybody is a critic.

Chapter Nine

The next day was Thursday, the best day of my week because it is my day off. There was no police patrol to run because the RVIPF commissioner prided himself on staying within his budget, and the budget provided for no overtime for special constables absent a state of emergency. In my twenty years as Anegada's sole RVIPF representative, I had never worked an hour of overtime. A state of emergency on Anegada was as likely as Her Majesty dropping by for a spot of tea and scones at the single table at Dotsey's Bakery. Come to think of it, a royal visit would probably be the only event the commissioner would consider worthy of declaring an emergency.

My shift at the electric plant began at midnight on Fridays, so the day was a true full day off. When we were first married, Icilda would make sure that her Thursday was unscheduled as well, allowing us time for a day at the beach at

Loblolly, a snorkeling trip to Horseshoe Reef, or a picnic at some lonesome strand on the north shore. Icilda had been as hungry for my body then as Cat was now, and our outings often ripened into an afternoon of lovemaking beneath Anegada's azure skies.

Those blissful times drifted away after Tamia came along, and Thursdays became just another workday for Icilda at the Reef Hotel, and a day for work around the house, or for gathering a few lobsters or conchs in the *Lily B*, for me. Or, for the last several months, a clandestine visit to an empty beach with Cat. But on this particular Thursday, she was scheduled to fly shuttle service from St. Thomas to San Juan, so I planned a conching expedition.

The sloping waist-deep flat inside Horseshoe Reef near the East End is home to thousands of conchs. The seemingly inexhaustible supply of the tasty shellfish is confirmed by the great bleached mounds of their shells heaped by Anegadians at the East Point over the years, first by the peaceful Arawaks; then by the Arawaks' conquerors, the Caribs; then by Dutch settlers, pirates, and sugar plantation slaves; and finally by the descendants of plantation slaves such as me. We had all followed the same course, diving in the shallow water for the mollusks, piercing their elegant shells near the tip to insert a knife and cut the muscle holding them in, discarding the shells with the thousands on the mounds, and stewing, frying, or eating raw the meat of the conch "foot."

A thousand years of this did not appear to have made a dent in the supply of conchs. It did make for a pleasant way to idle away an afternoon while seeming to be productive. Free diving in the clear waters on the hunt for tasty prey with an escape speed of three yards per hour, with timely breaks for a rest and a swig of rum, can hardly be matched as day-off amusement.

This Thursday was to be particularly special because I had persuaded Icilda to allow Kevin to play hooky from school for a father-son day on the water. I had not seen enough of my little man lately.

Kevin bolted his breakfast, wiped his mouth with the back of his hand after finishing his guava juice, and implored, "Hurry up, Dada."

"What's the rush, little man?" I said. "If the conch started to run a week ago, they still couldn't get away."

"We might miss something, Dada. A triggerfish, a whale, maybe even a shark!" Kevin said, eyes wide. It took me back, remembering the days when my dada would take me with him to go fishing or conching, just the two of us, free and easy on the wide green sea. "What if a shark comes after us?"

"I'll poke him on the snout with my poling stick. Besides, you have nothing to worry about. The shark won't want a bony little man like you. What is he going to do, pick his teeth with all those bones? There isn't enough of you for a decent shark meal."

"You wait, Dada. When I grow up I'll be big enough to wrestle the sharks and beat them with my bare hands."

"Well, let's just see if you can beat the conchs today." I laughed.

"Are we going to dive deep to get them, Dada?" Kevin was already a good swimmer, a comfortable young dolphin in the water.

"We'll go to the East End, as usual, but if you won't be scared, we can dive in Budrock Hole. The conchs are so thick on the bottom there you can't put down your feet without stepping on one."

"I won't be scared," Kevin said earnestly.

"And if we fill the boat and finish cleaning the meat soon enough, we can take some scraps out to the reef and do some fishing."

"Let's go, Dada!" Kevin was out the door.

I was loading gasoline, water, rum, and limes for a lunch of conch ceviche into the *Lily B* when the CB in the Land Rover barked with a call from Lawrence Vanterpool, proprietor of the Reef Hotel. Kevin waited eagerly in the skiff while I took the call. The honeymooners from yesterday's flight apparently craved nonstop action, Lawrence said. After he regaled me with a graphic description, including impersonations, of last night's emanations from the honeymoon suite, he informed me that he had sold the lovebirds my services as a fishing guide. The happy couple, now known to the hotel staff as "Mr. and Mrs. Yes, Yes! There, Yes! Oh, Faster, Yes!," or "Mr. and Mrs. Yes" for short, would meet me at the hotel dock in half an hour.

There was disappointment in Kevin's eyes when I told him our conching trip would have to wait, but he understood what we all understand on Anegada—tourist desires take priority over our own, even when it means a father-son outing must be put aside. The winter tourist season is short and opportunities to make money during that time must be seized. Icilda had lectured me on that very topic more than once in Kevin's presence. He nodded his solemn, man-to-man assent, and I sent him on his way to his grandparents' house, watching as he walked stoically down the dock and along the sand road. A year or two ago, there would have been a protest and maybe a tear, but not now. My little man was on his way to becoming a man.

Escape from the rigors of the honeymoon suite had to be the only explanation for the interest of Mr. and Mrs. Yes in fishing. They staggered onto the dock in a haze of bleary bliss, equipped only with bathing suits and enough sunscreen to shield them from a burn on the surface of Mercury. A quick inquiry about their fishing experience revealed it to be nil, so I decided stalking bonefish on the flats with eight-weight fly rods would make for a long afternoon and a small tip. Opting for a sure thing, we embarked on a West End mud run.

While bonefish on the flats are wary and usually gone before a novice even spots them, mudding bones are a guaranteed success for the first-time angler. Mudding occurs when a large school of the nearly transparent game fish stakes out an area of the bottom in ten to twelve feet of water, methodically rooting through the sand in search of crabs, worms, and other tidbits. The commotion on the bottom stirs up enough sand and silt to turn the normally air-clear water a milky shade of green-white. While the water is not truly muddy, it is the closest we come to it here on Anegada. Anything resembling a crab, shrimp, or worm dragged through a bonefish mud is immediately inhaled by one of the feeding fish, and the fight is on.

Veteran bonefish anglers disdain mudding as artless and crass. Mr. and Mrs. Yes, not knowing any better, delightedly caught slab after silvery slab of bonefish lightning on the bedraggled spinning outfits I kept in the gunwale locker for anglers with no tackle of their own.

At the end of two hours of nonstop fish fighting, Mr. and Mrs. Yes's biceps and triceps had undergone a workout equal to the one their nether regions had experienced the preceding night. They took a break as we drifted with the current off the sharply inclined beach at the West End. Mrs. Yes pointed out a rusting post and angle iron just above the tide line and asked what it was.

"It's from an old NASA tracking station," I explained. "From the late 1950s to the late 1960s, NASA had a downrange tracking station on Anegada. They used it to track the *Mercury* and *Gemini* spacecraft launches from Cape Canaveral. The post and angle iron are all that is left standing. If you explore the area onshore, you'll find some old pierced-steel planking laid in sheets to form a helicopter pad. All the buildings and other equipment were removed long before I was born, but my father told me the US Navy and Army used to helicopter in supplies and equipment for the station from Puerto Rico."

"The navy? I love the navy!" Mrs. Yes exclaimed cheerfully.

"I'll bet you do," Mr. Yes muttered sotto voce.

The chances of completing my conching trip with Kevin were gone by the time I deposited Mr. and Mrs. Yes at the Reef Hotel dock at midafternoon. They left a generous tip and, restored by the sun and fresh air, headed for another prolonged session in the bridal suite. At loose ends, I decided to go to the police station to see if there were any messages and maybe to get on the Internet if Pamela Pickering was not using the computer.

I walked into the empty police station ten minutes later. On my desk was a pink slip with a message to call Rollie Stoutt written in Pamela Pickering's childish scrawl. He picked up after one ring.

"Hello, Inspector Stoutt, it's Special Constable Creque returning your call."

"Constable, I called to see if you had any success in locating Paul Kelliher's next of kin yet. His autopsy has been completed, with the cause of death the single gunshot wound. The coroner is ready to release the body. Actually, he desperately needs to release the body. Space is tight in the morgue. He said no one has contacted him to make arrangements."

"I haven't located any next of kin yet," I said. "I don't think he was who his identification says he was. We may need to send a set of his fingerprints to the States to see if he can be identified that way. I have a contact in the Boston Police

Department, a Detective Sergeant Donovan, who is willing to help us with that. I can give him a call and you can follow up with a fax of the prints to him."

"Nothing to fax, Constable. The crabs and gulls ruined any chance for prints. Every digit was missing, or mutilated to such an extent that even partial prints are not available. What about information in the personal effects? Has that given you any leads?"

I thought about the coded notebook and decided against mentioning it to Rollie. I still had the intuition that nothing would be done about decoding it if I turned it over.

"Nothing," I lied.

"Well, keep trying. I'll do what I can here and let's stay in contact. Otherwise, Mr. Kelliher, or whoever he was, will end up in a pauper's grave in St. George's Cemetery."

"Yes, Inspector."

The weight of my lie did not seem counterbalanced by my motive to do good. Now I was lying to a superior officer about evidence in a criminal investigation. What was I becoming? Lies to Icilda, lies to Inspector Stoutt, the affair with Cat. My life was out of control. I was not cut out for this. But in a place like Anegada, you learn quickly that the only way out of your problems is to deal with them yourself, one at a time.

The problem I could do the most about at that moment was solving the mystery that was Paul Kelliher. I went to Pamela's office, walking past the paper sign on her door declaring that she would return on Friday. The Acer PC on her desk appeared to be more of a repository for sticky notes than a computer, and I had to excavate the grimy keyboard from the mounds of paper covering it. Firing up the machine, I logged in using her clever secret password, the ten single numerals on the keyboard, in order.

I do not know that much about computers and the Internet but there is really only one thing anyone needs to know—Google. Calling up the Google search box, I typed in "Paul Kelliher Boston University." The results showed nothing that linked that name to the institution. "Paul Kelliher biologist" got the same result. "Paul Kelliher PhD," "Paul Kelliher iguana," "Paul Kelliher Bonnie Kelliher," "Paul Kelliher obituary," and "Bonnie Kelliher obituary" all returned nothing that seemed even remotely connected to the body in the Road Town morgue.

The late afternoon sun slanted in the windows, filling the office with drowsy heat. A gecko sat motionless on the windowsill. My mind drifted and I idly searched "Mary Catherine Wells." There she was on the "Our Pilots" page of the VI Birds Air Charters website, her confident grin much more suited for public consumption than the erotic smile she reserved for me. Another site contained a report of her departure to the Virgin Islands from her position as a helicopter traffic reporter for KTRH NewsRadio 740 in Houston.

But the most interesting find was a 2011 article from the online edition of the *Houston Chronicle*, reporting on the twentieth anniversary of Operation Desert Storm. It described the roles of local veterans, including Cat, in the conflict.

Under the heading "Cat Wells follows in Her Father's Footsteps," the reporter wrote:

> Local KTRH traffic reporter Mary Catherine "Cat" Wells received a baptism by fire as a US Army helicopter pilot in Desert Storm. The daughter of retired army chief warrant officer Neville Wells, Cat grew up at army bases around the world, including Germany, Hawaii, Japan, and Puerto Rico. On graduating from high school, she enlisted in the army "to fly helicopters just like [her] dad."
>
> At a time when women's roles in the army were still evolving, Cat Wells became one of its first female combat aviators. Less than six months after completing her flight training at age 22, she was sent to Illesheim, Germany, to join the Second Squadron of the Sixth Cavalry as its first female Apache helicopter pilot.
>
> When the "Fighting Sixth" deployed to Saudi Arabia in 1991, Wells found herself involved in the conflict for which she and the rest of the $2/6^{th}$ would receive the Valorous Unit Award from the Secretary of the Army. Flying in all of the combat missions of the $2/6^{th}$ during the war, she was personally responsible for the destruction of a dozen Iraqi armored vehicles, including four tanks.
>
> "It was tough at first, being the only female pilot in my unit. Some of the older guys grumbled about

having a 'lady pilot' on their wing if it all hit the fan. But when combat finally began, we all worked together and no one worried about having me as their wingman," she said.

The camaraderie of the unit is evident in the photo of the 2/6th pilots below. Taken on the day hostilities ceased, Wells is shown carrying the same sidearm that her father wore in Vietnam.

"The standard-issue sidearm for helicopter crews at that time was the Beretta nine-millimeter, but I always carried my dad's Smith & Wesson .38. He gave it to me just before I left on my first deployment, and it always felt like he was there protecting me when I wore it," Wells said. Sadly, her father died only two days after this photo was taken.

Cat Wells served ten years as an army aviator before returning to civilian life as Houston's Traffic Eye at KTRH in 2000. While she enjoys her work in civilian life, she misses the excitement of flying for the army. As she put it, "Civilian life is safe and routine, but nothing makes you feel more alive than heading out on a mission where you don't know what you will encounter and how you will overcome it."

Below the article was a photograph of seven men and Cat. The stark tan of the desert made up the foreground and background color, with a cloudless sky overhead. The eight stood in front of a lethal-looking helicopter bristling with weapons.

All were dressed in desert camouflage fatigues. Some carried sidearms strapped to their thighs or in shoulder holsters. Their boots were dusty, as if they had defeated Saddam Hussein's army by marching against it, rather than flying. All wore smiles of relief, smiles of success and victory, smiles at the prospect of going home. In the grainy two-decade-old photograph, Cat's appearance was essentially the same as now. She still wore her hair cropped close and her face was still unlined and youthful.

I did not know until then that Cat had distinguished herself in Desert Storm. She had touched on it briefly but had downplayed her role and seemed reluctant to discuss it. I suppose when you have killed in combat it is not something you wish to relive. I was also surprised to learn she had lived in Puerto Rico when she was growing up. She had never mentioned it, though San Juan is only about a hundred miles away. Sometimes Cat seemed to be only slightly less a mystery than Paul Kelliher.

Chapter Ten

The hours spent on Pamela Pickering's computer felt like fishing without catching any fish, except it took place in the quiet box of an office without the benefit of the lambent sun and warm waters of the flats. I decided to head home, with a stop at the Methodist church on the way to see if Anthony Wedderburn was having better luck than me.

Stepping into the monastic quiet of the Thursday-afternoon church was disconcerting. I had not crossed the threshold of the little church on many Thursdays, or other days for that matter, in the last few years. I was especially adept at avoiding Sundays, despite the inevitable admonition about the destination of my immortal soul from a disapproving Icilda.

Anthony was seated with his back to me at a long narrow table normally used for hymnals. He had placed the hymnals in neat stacks in the nearest pew. The table was covered with a chaotic array of working papers, over which he hunched absorbed in concentration.

"Good afternoon, Anthony."

My greeting seemed to pull Anthony gradually to the surface from someplace very deep. As he turned, his eyes hesitated for a moment as their focus changed from the page before him to my face. He smiled, not the goofy, ganja-induced smile he had worn since the first day we met, but the genuine smile of a man greeting a good friend. The pupils of his eyes were normal, and the whites were not their usual web of red veins. He sat up straight and squared his shoulders. He was clean-shaven. His blond dreadlocks were washed and as neat as dreadlocks can ever be. He was no longer De White Rasta. He was a man with a purpose.

"Delightful to see you, Teddy. I am making good progress here. I should have this thing cracked in another day or two. Honestly, this is the most fun I have had in years." Anthony's public school accent did not seem as out of place coming from his mouth as it once had.

"Have you broken the code, or some part of it?" I asked. I was hoping for a hint of success to prevent the morning excursion with Mr. and Mrs. Yes from being the highlight of my day.

"Here, Teddy, have a look. I have one line. I picked it out of the middle of the book. I just had a feeling I might be able to knock it." Anthony shoved a paper from the pile in front of him into my hand.

On the back of last month's church bulletin, Anthony

had scribbled a long single line of letters followed by the same letters broken into four rows angling across the page. The letters in the first row were in parentheses:

(H) (W) (S) (E) (F) (O) (H) (A) (T) (F) (O)

A R 5 X L 3 H D V U 9

9 E N B 1 P T 4 G Y I

E A W T R M E D O O T

"It turns out the middle two rows are dead rows, so the 'rail fence' is the first and the last row only, like so." Anthony quickly put parentheses on the letters of the bottom row and then wrote out the combined first and last rows in the order they appeared. He placed slashes between some of the letters:

H E / W A S / W E T / F R O M / H E A D / T O / F O O T

"Not bad for a blackheart man, eh, Teddy? It was a bit of a rough go at the start; I had some trouble with focus. But now that I have some of the cobwebs cleared away, I shan't be long with the rest. It is a simple matter of figuring out the pattern of dead rows. There is probably a repeating sequence of numbers." Anthony beamed and continued, "Give me two days to work out the dead-row sequence and it will be cracked. Any idea about the meaning of what I have so far?"

"I wish I had some idea, Anthony, but nothing comes immediately to mind."

"Well, cheerio. I am certain it will all be clear soon."

Anthony turned back to his scattered papers. I was obviously being dismissed by a busy man hard at work, so I headed home.

Icilda was at the stove when I walked through the door, her sturdy bulk obscuring the food she was cooking. I had not eaten since breakfast and the smell made me realize how hungry I was. Icilda had always been a great cook. I hugged her and glanced over her shoulder. Pumpkin soup, sweet potatoes and onions, and fried grouper fingers.

She shrugged me off. “Where you been, Teddy?”

I gave her the sanitized version of my day. “Had a fishing charter from the hotel, then went to the police station to do a little work, and then stopped in at the church.”

“The church? I can’t get you there for the Sunday service but you go there on your day off in the middle of the week?”

“I was checking up on Anthony Wedderburn.”

“I saw De Rasta there yesterday when I stopped to pick up the lesson for the Ladies’ Circle,” she said. “He was over in the corner by himself. He seemed . . . cleaner. What is going on with him? Did you persuade him to go to church, Teddy?”

“He is helping me with something and we decided that the church would be a nice quiet place to work.”

Unlike Cat, Icilda did not seem to think it unusual that De Rasta would be working with me. Instead, her thoughts immediately leaped to the possibility of saving Lord Wedderburn’s soul.

"Has this work you have given him inspired him to change his ways? Should I talk to Pastor Lloyd about helping him to accept Jesus as his Savior?" There was fervor in Icilda's voice heard only on the not-infrequent occasions when she mentioned Jesus and Pastor Lloyd in the same sentence.

"I think he may need to do some soul-searching of his own before he is ready to speak to the pastor. I'll let you know when the time is right." I hoped this would be enough to keep Icilda from siccing the slightly effeminate Pastor Lloyd and his stable of earnest church ladies on De Rasta. At least until the work on the notebook was complete.

The dodge seemed to work; Icilda shifted her inquiry. "What kind of work is De Rasta doing for you? I've never known him to do work of any kind, outside of cultivating his shag patch."

"He's helping me on the murder case. He is working on decoding a notebook I found in the victim's personal effects. He said he has some expertise with that kind of thing and I'm hoping it will help in finding the killer."

"I thought you were off the case?" Icilda concentrated on ladling the soup into bowls, despite the question in her inflection.

"I'm doing a little investigating on my own to see if I can help."

Icilda turned from her soup, brandishing the ladle like a weapon. She had an angry frown that seemed to appear more often lately on her face. "On your own? Are you sure you should be doing that, Teddy? We need you to keep that job.

Aren't you in enough trouble with the deputy commissioner already?"

She was right. I knew she was right. I told her she was right, that it was an unnecessary risk to my job. I told her I would stop investigating and leave the job to the professionals in Road Town.

I lied. I deceived Icilda about stopping my investigation, just as I deceived her about Cat Wells, just as I deceived Rollie Stoutt about the notebook, just as I deceived Cat about going on with our relationship. I did it because deception was easier than fighting the fight, easier than explaining myself, easier than facing my guilt. I bought peace with this deception, as I did with all my deceptions, knowing the peace was temporary and the day of reckoning would come.

After dinner, I sat in the quiet outside, listening to the chatter between Icilda and Tamia as they did the dinner dishes, and thinking about how easily deceit and duplicity came to me these days.

It was not a pleasant way to pass the evening.

Chapter Eleven

It rained during the night, a gentle, steady rain, the kind of rain that is always a surprise on Anegada, where most rains are either a quick burst from a squall or an apocalyptic three-day deluge accompanied by the frightening beast that is a hurricane. The rain was gone by sunrise, the air washed clear and clean.

My dark mood had been cleansed by the rain as well. I hummed Bob Marley's "Sun Is Shining" as I began my routine patrol circuit driving west from The Settlement. The *Bomba Charger*, on its thrice-a-week run from Tortola, was due to arrive just after eight a.m., so the government dock at Setting Point was my first stop.

Leaning against the hood of the Land Rover watching the ferry passengers disembark, I pondered the next step in the investigation in which I had now promised everyone but my mother that I would not participate. By the time the last passenger drifted away, I had come to the realization that I had no leads in the case. The only reasonable course was to wait for Anthony Wedderburn to finish deciphering the notebook and hope its contents would give some direction.

Having abandoned reason several days ago, I decided to use my patrol to retrace some of the steps I had already taken and see if there was something I had missed along the way. I would begin by visiting Wendell George. Maybe he could make sense out of the single decoded line of Kelliher's notebook.

I eased the Land Rover through the sand parking area at the Pomato Point Restaurant, using low gear and taking care to avoid the particularly soft parts. The long straight beach to the west of the building was devoid of human presence. A black-hulled catamaran was anchored, fore and aft, a few yards offshore. There was no one on its deck. A lizard on the hunt for a tasty fly breakfast was the only sign of life as I walked up the three tiled steps into the shaded interior of the restaurant. It took a moment for my eyes to adjust.

The Mistress was across the room, stretching to dust the bottles on the high shelving behind the bar. She hummed as she worked, "La Vie en Rose," her voice throaty and rich as a velvet robe. Humming seemed to be the order of the day.

I cleared my throat, hoping not to startle her.

"Good morning, Constable. A fine morning, isn't it?" She spoke while continuing her dusting. It was the first time I had ever heard her speak and I realized what I had been missing all these years. The rich contralto in which she had hummed was married with a breathy island French accent, possibly from Martinique. My thoughts strayed to the seedy decay of Fort-de-France, black coffee and Cointreau, and making love in the afternoon. How did Wendell manage to keep his mind on treasure?

"A fine morning, indeed, Miss . . . eh," I hesitated, realizing that we had never been introduced and I did not know her name.

"Marie. Please call me Marie, Constable."

I would have called her the queen of Sheba if the request came in that intoxicating tone.

"I suppose you are looking for Wendell," she continued.

"Yes . . . Marie." After so many years of her silence, learning her name and speaking it for the first time made me feel excited and somehow ashamed at the same time.

"Wendell is gone. Wendell is *toujours* gone since you came with the maps and the notebook. He hunts the treasure. Every day he is gone before the sun is up. Every night he returns after the sun is down. He goes far out to the East End. He is there now, with his shovels, and his compass, and his detector of metals. He is exhausted, but he is up half the night, plotting on his maps. He thinks there is a treasure and he thinks he knows where it is but he finds *rien*, nothing. He digs and digs, *comme un fou*, like a crazy man. He will tire of it before he finds a thing, because there is not a thing to find." She had a great deal more to say today than she ever had before, but she did not seem upset or angry, just resigned.

"Why do you say there is nothing to find?" The question

came out as a reaction, spoken before I thought about whether it was important. Just another example of my clever police work.

"The Professor Kelliher, he search and dig for how long? *Cinq ans*, five years, eh? And Wendell, his whole life with his detector of metals, to find what? A musket ball here, a nail there, a handful of coins. If there was this treasure to be found, Wendell would have found it, or this professor would have found it, in all this searching. There is no treasure; there is no thing to find. There is only the foolish *avarice*, the greed." She shook her head, the soft curls framing her face bouncing like orchids in the breeze.

"If not for treasure, why would someone kill Paul Kelliher?" I asked, as if she had the answer.

"Yes, yes, why? Why search out this professor, go out to the Spanish Camp from . . . where? From Tortola? Or does this killer come from further? The US? South America? Europe? Why come so far to kill a man? I have not this answer but my people have *un proverbe*, this what you call . . . saying, when you wish to know *pourquoi*, when you wish to know why . . . *cherchez la femme*. Look for the woman. There may not be any treasure but there is a woman in this mystery you try to solve. There always is. Look for the woman and the rest will show itself to you, Constable."

Marie brought her eyes up to meet mine with a cool, steady gaze. I know what you are thinking, but it was not that kind of gaze. And besides, I already had my plate completely full in that arena. No, Marie's eyes unfailingly told me to get out there and find the woman and her role in this mystery, and not to be a disappointment to her like Wendell. Taking a page from the Mistress's book, I nodded silently and took my leave.

As I turned toward the West End, a glint of morning sun on the outrageous mango yellow of a VI Birds helicopter flying low over the water caught my eye. As customs officer, I would have been notified in advance if a landing was intended, so its passengers were probably some folks with money to burn on an aerial sightseeing tour of the BVI. There were several helicopter pilots at VI Birds, but I imagined that Cat was at the stick and wondered whether the tour she gave would include the beaches and bays where we had made love. The copter crossed from water to land, staying low, less than fifty feet off the deck, and didn't seem to be in a touring mode, making a direct line for the airport. Maybe the passengers were coming from Tortola and did not need to clear customs. I decided to check in at the airport as my patrol took me around the island.

As I rounded the turn at the West End, the road was completely blocked by seven scrawny cattle. Rather than nudge them with the Land Rover, I stopped and waited for them to amble out of the way. I thought about Marie's suggestion. A strategy of *cherchez la femme* might give some much-needed new direction to my stalled investigation. But a moment's thought made me realize that not only were there no women associated with Paul Kelliher's death, there were no human beings whatsoever known to be involved, unless you counted

De White Rasta coming upon the body, and I could not bring myself to consider him a suspect. There was no wife, no girlfriend, and no other man's woman in the picture. The only woman who could even be placed with Kelliher was Belle Lloyd, his only real contact on Anegada. The road took me directly past Cow Wreck Bay. *Cherchez la femme*, I thought. Here I go.

Friday is usually restful and quiet on Anegada. Bareboat charters in the BVI end on Saturdays at noon, and the sailors usually head back to Tortola for a hard-partying Friday night before turning in their boats the next morning. This means a boat exodus from Anegada each Friday morning at dawn, or as soon after as hangovers will allow, and Anegada for the Anegadians until the following Tuesday or Wednesday, when the new crop of sailors arrives.

This particular Friday was true to form. When I entered the Cow Wreck Beach Bar and Grill shortly before noon, the bar was empty. The only sign of life, if it could be called that, was the fiftysomething vacationer in a Speedo on the beach, being delicately broiled by the midday sun. Belle was nowhere to be seen but I heard some rustling from the storage lean-to at the back of the bar. I found Belle on her knees near the cot she had kept for Paul Kelliher, stuffing something into a trash bag. She started as she saw me when she turned to get up.

"Oh, Teddy, you are going to be my death sneaking up like that." Belle placed her hand on her chest and closed her eyes for a moment to compose herself.

"Sorry, Belle, I didn't mean to startle you. Slow morning?"

"Just Mr. Too Much Flesh, Not Enough Speedo out on the sand. Complains about prices. Complains about no German beer. I got Heineken, ain't that close enough? I decided to do some cleaning back here rather than just sit and watch all that pale skin go from baby pink to lobster red. You here for lunch?" Belle placed the garbage bag off to the side and stepped between me and it as she spoke.

"Not today, Belle. What are you getting rid of? Not any of Kelliher's things, I hope?"

"No . . . no. There are none of his things left here. You took them all with you last week." Belle's hands flitted in a nervous gesture toward the bag. "Just some old odds and ends I need to clean out of here."

"Like what, Belle? Mind if I take a look in the bag?" My curiosity was piqued. Was there something in the bag that Belle did not want me to see?

Belle frowned. "Yes, I do mind. Are you saying I'm holding back something about Professor Kelliher, Teddy? Are you suspecting me of something? After I treat you like a son? After I fed you all those lunches? You come into my own place and get all po-lice-man with me after I been so good to you? I don't hide anything from you but I don't have to take this from you, constable or not. Come into my own bar and insult me."

"Belle, don't be this way. I'm just trying to do my job."

"So you do think I am hiding something from you?" Belle huffed.

"Well . . . if I could just look in the bag."

"Get out of my place," Belle said, bristling with anger. "Get out, and when you come back to accuse me and search the next time, you better have a search warrant from a magistrate, not just be on some damn fishing expedition." Glaring at me, Belle seized the garbage bag.

Belle was within her rights to refuse to let me look in the bag. She was within her rights to order me to leave. And there was no way I could get a search warrant from a magistrate for an investigation I had been expressly ordered not to conduct. I did the only thing I could do. I left. When I looked in my rearview mirror as I drove out of the crushed-coral parking lot, Belle was standing at the entrance to the bar, hands on hips, making sure of my departure.

My regular patrol route followed the two ruts of sand road that ran parallel to the north shore. As I did on every patrol, I drove down the side paths to the beaches at Keel Point, Bones Bight, and Windlass Bight. A check with binoculars at each beach revealed nothing but the sea, the gulls, and the occasional wading cow. Lingering at Windlass, I ruminated over the falling-out with Belle. Here was a person I had known for years and seen almost daily. Why had she suddenly been so defensive? Had I been so ham-handed with my questions as to cause someone I considered a friend to be offended? Or did she really have something to conceal?

My eyes tracked the flight of a pelican as it skimmed the water, abruptly rose, and then folded its wings into a dive. When the bird bobbed to the surface, the tail of a sprat poked out of its bill for a moment before being tipped down its gullet; pretty simple and straightforward for both the pelican and the sprat. Why couldn't it be as simple and straightforward for me? Just go to Belle, ask the questions, and get the answers. Solve the crime of Kelliher's murder, and go back to life as it was, no disruptions, no turmoil, easy days and quiet nights. Back to the rhythm of my life. Maybe that was what set Belle off, my disruption of the quiet rhythm of her life.

It was not fair to Belle, though, to think what I wanted was also her desire. It dawned on me that there was a simple and straightforward explanation for her anger. It was because I had treated her as a suspect. And without any basis in fact, just because I thought she was acting furtively with the bag of trash. Was she really, objectively, acting as if she had something to hide? Not objectively, until I had all but accused her. And why had I done that? Because the Mistress purred "*cherchez la femme*" at me and I was not smart enough to actually develop real evidence and uncover real clues. In short, Belle was angry at me because I was an incompetent policeman.

A competent policeman, I realized, would have no reason to suspect Belle. She had cooperated fully when I had come to her for information on Paul Kelliher, told me what she knew and turned over his belongings to me, including the maps and what might turn out to be my best clue, the coded notebook. Paul Kelliher's killer would not have done that. And Belle had no motive and, to my knowledge, no gun to carry out the crime. I decided I owed her an apology.

I backed the Land Rover around and drove toward the main road. Stopping where the beach path met the twin ruts of the road, I glimpsed a flash of mango yellow low on the horizon.

The VI Birds helicopter appeared to have just lifted off from the airport. Staying low, it took a direct course over Flamingo Pond, toward the sea and the US Virgin Islands. Thinking I might still encounter any passengers who had disembarked at the airport, I turned east. My apology to Belle would have to wait until tomorrow.

The loop road along the north shore meets the airport road at one of the three actual intersections on Anegada. In any other place, there would be a stop sign or traffic light. On Anegada, the two sand paths simply meet at a right angle. Turn south and you pass the airport and eventually reach The Settlement. Turn northeast and in a couple of miles the road tops the low dune at Loblolly Bay and ends.

I had intended to turn south at the intersection but the thinnest pall of road dust hung motionless in the air to the northeast. Whoever had landed at the airport had already driven off toward Loblolly. I turned northeast and in less than a quarter mile spotted the source of the dust parked in the circular driveway of Frangipani House.

Chapter Twelve

Frangipani House is something of an aberration for Anegada. The only residence built anywhere north of the east-west axis of the island, it is one of only two properties here that could aptly be called "high-end." Constructed in the late 1970s by the third wife of a British record executive as her post-divorce refuge, it boasts modernist styling and the island's only swimming pool.

When the divorcée's ex-husband went bankrupt and the alimony payments dried up, the house was the only hard asset for her creditors to squabble over. The litigation took just short of a decade on the glacial docket of the high court in Road Town. Frangipani House was finally sold at auction and then passed through the hands of a series of owners until the present pair, a fashion designer from New Jersey and his FDNY firefighter husband. They had restored Frangipani

House to its full disco-era chic and now rented it out by the week or month.

The white Mitsubishi Montero parked at the front door was one of two rental cars owned by Donnie Vanterpool's Car Rentals. Cat Wells's shapely backside jutted enticingly from its open hatch as I wheeled into the drive.

Hearing the sound of my tires, Cat turned and set a box of groceries on the ground.

"The cops on this island don't miss a thing," she complained playfully, pursing her lips in their best seductive pout.

"Just doing my job, ma'am," I said, playing along. "After all, I am the customs officer for Anegada and a special constable for the Royal Virgin Islands Police Force."

The reprise of my officious greeting from the first day we met drew a repeat of Cat's formal snap to attention and salute. This time, though, I managed to not crack a smile.

"You are required to clear customs at the airport, ma'am." I kept a facetious edge to my voice but maybe I was a little serious. Why had she not checked in?

"Oh, I am so sorry, officer." She leaned in against me, looking up through long lashes, a hand on my chest. "I didn't mean to cause a problem."

"Well, don't let it happen again," I kept on. "Are you a visitor or a belonger?"

"A visitor to your fair island."

"How long do you intend to stay, ma'am?"

"I have rented Frangipani House for a week."

"And what is the purpose of your visit, business or pleasure?"

"I came over to surprise my boyfriend. He's a handsome stud, so I guess you could say . . . pleasure. My pleasure and his. Do you think he'll enjoy the surprise?"

I never had a chance to answer. She dropped her hand to unbutton my uniform pants and took me there in the driveway. And again, in the massive mahogany four-poster bed upstairs. And again, on the kitchen counter in the late afternoon when we went downstairs for a drink of water.

Suddenly it was four o'clock. I hurried out to meet a sailboat arriving from Antigua scheduled to be at the government dock at three. I would have to stamp Cat's passport later.

After mumbling about "island time" to the irate sailors and seeing that they had left Antigua on the day after Paul Kelliher had been found dead, I passed them through customs with a perfunctory glance at their passports and luggage.

The sun was half gone on the horizon by the time I pointed the RVIPF Land Rover toward The Settlement. I was exhausted from the afternoon with Cat. My nether regions ached. Cat had the sexual appetite of a debauched nun trying to make up for lost time. I worried that I was going to be called on to perform this way every day for the next week. A quiet evening at home was what I needed.

My daily patrol always ended with a slow tour along the one paved street of The Settlement. After a few minutes chatting with the tough boys wearing out the pool table at

Cardi's, it was full dark. Here and there light escaped from a curtained window, but my headlights were the only lights on the street. I decided to swing by the Methodist church to see if Anthony Wedderburn had made any progress.

Even before driving into the parking area in front of the church, I could tell Anthony was not there. There was no light showing through any of the shutters on the building. I leaned from my window and listened for a moment; there was only silence. I decided I would catch up with De Rasta in the morning. I would be fresher then, anyway.

When I arrived home, the house was dark save for a light in the kitchen, where Tamia sat at the table with a worksheet paper, a pencil, an open math book, and a forlorn look on her face.

"Hi, Dada," she said.

"Hello, sweet dawta, where's your madda?"

"She got called to work the dinner shift at the hotel. Lorraine Penn has the flu. She said she'll be home by eleven."

"And little man Kevin?"

"He's sleeping over at Mullet Soares's house."

"An' why do you have that horse look on your face, sweet dawta?" Tamia softened at being called by her baby name for the second time.

"This old algebra is not gonna do me any good. Why do I have to learn it?"

"That's so when you are a full-grown lady like your madda and old and hairy like your dada you can work with your mind instead of waiting tables and catching smelly fish for a living. Now, show me what has you stuck."

Tamia sighed the signature sigh of all teenagers and explained. We pored over the worksheet together, smiling at each other when our heads bumped. My thoughts flashed back to when I first held her in my hands, so small and fragile, and swore to myself that I would protect her from the world. She is a smart child and it only took a bit of prompting and an encouraging word for her to grasp the necessary concept and complete the worksheet.

"Thanks, Dada. You're the best," she said, and planted a little-girl peck on my cheek. Then she asked, "Dada, are you all right?"

"Fine, sweet dawta, just a little tired." Thank the Lord she did not ask why. "Off to bed for both of us now." Three minutes later I slipped between the cool sheets, finally falling into a fitful sleep after an hour. I didn't awaken until Icilda shook my shoulder at midnight and wordlessly slid into bed as I got out the other side to go to my late shift at the power plant.

The diesels at the plant were cooperative, their even hum providing a lullaby sweet and soothing as any mother's melody. I woke from my cot in the generator room just as Jimmy Lloyd arrived for the day shift.

Since I had missed Anthony Wedderburn on yesterday's patrol, I took the chance that he would be getting an early start at the church. I was anxious about his progress in deciphering Paul Kelliher's notebook. He had promised to finish in a couple of days, and it had to be the break I needed on the case.

Otherwise, I had nowhere to turn.

Chapter Thirteen

The little Methodist church is as picturesque as any building on Anegada. Set off by itself on the northeast edge of The Settlement, it shares a shaded yard with a cemetery filled with past parishioners. Its cream stucco walls are punctuated by glassless shuttered windows that are opened to the trade winds during services. A single stained glass window depicting Christ on the Cross graces the wall behind the simple torchwood altar.

Several of the shutters were open, indicating someone was inside. As I mounted the two front steps in the warm morning air, the quiet of the churchyard was broken only by the chatter of a bananaquit. Pushing open the heavy wooden door revealed an interior bathed in golden light filtering through the stained glass window. It was impressive and welcoming at the same time, the Sistine Chapel of rustic Anegada.

The seated figure of De White Rasta was hunched over the hymnal table to the left of the altar, in much the same position as when I had left him two days before.

"Good morning, Anthony," I called as I approached between the two rows of pews.

There was no response to my greeting, which I attributed to deep concentration by De Rasta on his work. Then I saw the blood, spread thick on the table and in a pool at his feet. The blood was dry, a cold black smear across the sunlit floor, a cold black hand that reached into my chest and seized my heart.

"Oh, no, Anthony," I heard myself say. I ran to his side and felt his neck for a pulse. There was a faint throb, a murmur of life force in a body with the appearance of death. His skin was gray-pale beneath its tan, dry and almost cool. He leaned forward against the edge of the table, his right arm outstretched. A pen lay in the coagulated gore close to his curled fingers. His head hung a few inches above the table surface, a wide trail of dry blood running from his chin up to the ugly wound on the top of his skull.

A shattered branch of staghorn coral, bleached white as bone, lay scattered about the table and floor. The fragments of coral were thick as the handle of a cricket bat, matching the size of the concave groove in Anthony's cranium. Flakes of coral embedded in his blond dreadlocks confirmed that the branch had been the weapon. His assailant had probably picked it up from the flower beds outside the church, where the coral limbs were used as a border.

The heavy end of the staghorn branch, which would bear fingerprints, was missing. Tossing it out on any beach on the island, where it would blend with thousands of similar fragments littering the shore, would guarantee that it would never be discovered.

Judging from his position at the table and the pen fallen from his grasp, Anthony had been struck from behind as he worked on the coded notebook. The notebook and his work papers were nowhere to be seen.

Anthony was breathing on his own, and the bleeding from his wound had obviously stopped long ago. Still, it was apparent that he needed medical help as soon as possible. I scooped him up in my arms, intending to transport him somewhere to obtain that help. Where was not certain. The clinic at the administration building was closed; the rotating nurse who staffed it one day a week was in Virgin Gorda.

Pastor Lloyd chose that moment to enter the church. He had made his way down most of the center aisle before he stopped short, seeing his church turned into an abattoir. His audible gasp, followed by "Dear Lord, Teddy, what has happened here?" alerted me to his presence.

"Someone tried to kill Anthony. I have to get him to a hospital. Don't touch anything," I cautioned as I carried De Rasta past him.

"Tried to kill him . . . here, in the house of God?" the pastor whimpered, as if the location made the bludgeoning more heinous.

"I'm afraid the house of God is now a crime scene, Pastor.

Come outside and don't close the door or touch it on your way out," I called as I stumbled down the front steps.

Anthony was limp, nearly lifeless in my arms. He seemed to weigh no more than a bird. I had brought this upon him. I was momentarily taken back to my last meeting with De Rasta, remembering his joy and enthusiasm in helping with the coded notebook.

After gently lowering Anthony across the rear passenger seats of the Land Rover, I radioed for Pamela Pickering. For once she was at work, and didn't quibble or question when I ordered her to call VI Birds to get a plane, any plane, to Anegada to transport Anthony to the hospital in Tortola.

Anthony was still unconscious on the floor of the airport terminal when the VI Birds Piper Aztec taxied to a halt outside an hour later. Pamela had outdone herself; a nurse from Peebles Hospital sat in the copilot's seat and the two rear seats had been removed and replaced with a stretcher. An ambulance would be waiting to meet the plane on the runway when it returned to Tortola.

A few minutes later, I stood at the edge of the tarmac as the Aztec lifted off into the morning sun. I followed its flight as it turned south, until tears blurred my vision.

Chapter Fourteen

After her calls to VI Birds and Peebles Hospital, Pamela Pickering had made a third call to RVIPF headquarters, which generated an immediate and, for the RVIPF, massive response. In little more than two hours, the *St. Ursula* could be seen approaching the government dock, up on plane at full throttle, a quarter mile of frothing wake scarring the sea behind it. Deputy Commissioner Lane stood at his usual position in the bow, but now he was flanked by four burly police officers wearing sidearms. The helmsman also stood at the wheel. Only Rollie Stoutt was seated, clinging to the coaming in the stern, surrounded by his forensic equipment cases.

The helmsman cut the throttle mere yards from the dock, and the DC and the four officers piled ashore like the US Marines assaulting Iwo Jima. Their haste was for naught.

They were forced to mill about aimlessly while Rollie fussed and fiddled his way ashore with his gear.

With Inspector Stoutt finally disembarked, we crowded into the Land Rover, the deputy commissioner silent in the passenger seat, Rollie and two hulks jammed in the rear seat with the aluminum equipment cases, and the remaining two officers standing on the running boards, clinging grimly to the roof rack during the short ride to The Settlement.

The four officers automatically deployed to the four corners of the Methodist church when we halted in the parking area. Pastor Lloyd stood agog just outside the church door. Several passersby stopped and stared. This was the most police activity, indeed the most government activity, that Anegada's citizens had seen since the Maritime Regiment had hunted down the pirate Bone in 1681.

The deputy commissioner wasted no time approaching the church entrance and Pastor Lloyd. Drawing himself to full height, he focused on the pastor. "Good morning, sir. And you are?"

"Pastor Lloyd. This is my church." The pastor seemed to shrink a little as he said each word.

"Pastor, I am Deputy Commissioner Howard Lane of the Royal Virgin Islands Police Force. Your church is, unfortunately, a crime scene and under the authority and control of the RVIPF until further notice. Did you see what happened here?" the DC boomed in a voice that was one part Barry White, one part Sean Connery, and a smattering of God. The Old Testament version.

"No, Deputy Commissioner. I wasn't aware anything had happened until I stopped in to do some work this morning and found Teddy—er, Constable Creque—inside with poor Anthony Wedderburn."

"Did you see anyone here last night or this morning?"

"Just Constable Creque, this morning, as I said."

"Did you hear anything unusual—strange noises, raised voices—last night or this morning?"

"No, nothing."

"Who has access to the church other than you?"

"Well, I guess you could say everyone."

"Everyone?"

"The house of the Lord is open to all." Pastor Lloyd gestured with his arms held wide.

"Let me put it this way. Who has a key, Pastor?"

"No one. We do not lock the door. I don't know anyone who locks their doors on Anegada."

"Perhaps the good people of Anegada should unlearn that habit in light of recent events," the DC said. "Do you know the victim?"

"Everyone on Anegada knows De White Rasta." Noticing the DC's exasperated frown at his slightly unresponsive answer, the pastor quickly continued, "To answer your question, yes, I know him. He is often around The Settlement. Sometimes he sleeps in the church, if we have a stretch of weather where the nights are cool."

"De White Rasta?" The DC twitched a brow.

"That is Mr. Wedderburn's nickname. Everyone calls

him that because of his dreadlocks and the way he speaks. I daresay most folks around here do not know his real name."

"Does he have any enemies?"

"No."

"No arguments with anyone, no disputes or problems?"

"No, Deputy Commissioner. Anthony has a Christian attitude and is a friend to all. I have hope for his salvation. If not for that demon marijuana . . ." The pastor pronounced it *mar-i-hu-a-na*, like the name of an exotic tropical disease. In De Rasta's case, maybe it was.

"Does he buy marijuana or other drugs from anyone?"

"I do not know. I never actually saw him using marijuana but many times I saw him under its influence."

"Does he sell drugs to anyone?"

"Not that I am aware." Pastor Lloyd would not have been aware if half the matrons in the Ladies' Circle fired up a joint during their Wednesday evening prayer meeting.

"Where does he get his marijuana? Does he grow it himself?"

"Again, Deputy Commissioner, I do not know."

"Did he know Paul Kelliher, the man who was recently killed at Spanish Camp?"

"Anthony knows everyone, and everyone knows him. So I assume he did, but I have no direct knowledge of this," the pastor said primly.

"You are a font of information, Pastor," the DC growled.

"You are most welcome, Deputy Commissioner Lane,"

Pastor Lloyd replied, the DC's irony lost on him. With an abbreviated bow, he made a beeline for the parsonage.

The DC glared after him and muttered generally in Rollie Stoutt's direction, "There has to be a drug angle to this assault, and the murder. A druggie like Wedderburn supposedly finds Kelliher's body and then winds up beaten himself mere days later. I'll bet my last dollar there is a connection between the two men and narcotics. Have you turned up anything to indicate that Kelliher was involved in the drug trade?"

Maybe it was a desire to stand up for the only thing Anthony Wedderburn had left, his reputation. Maybe I didn't want to be caught omitting information like I had been at my last crime scene. Or maybe it was a subconscious need to accelerate and finalize the suspended suspension the DC had left hanging over my head. Whatever the reason, I piped up. "I don't think the assault on Anthony had anything to do with drugs."

"Oh, really, Special Constable?" Both of the DC's bushy brows stood at attention. "Why don't you provide us with your insight?"

"Anthony was working on a project for me. He was deciphering a coded notebook I found in Paul Kelliher's personal effects. He was using the church as a workplace and was close to breaking the code. When I found him this morning, the notebook and all of his work papers were gone. Whoever beat him did it to get the notebook, either to use it themselves or to prevent me from learning what was in it.

And I do not believe the notebook had anything to do with drug trafficking."

I paused to catch my breath. I had spilled the information rapidly, like a kid confessing to raiding the cookie jar and wanting it to be over quickly.

"Go on," said the DC, his measured tone mimicking the father waiting to hear the full cookie confession before applying the rod.

"Kelliher was not a biologist. Boston University, which he claimed was his employer, has no record of him. His address and the information in his passport are false. He wasn't here to study the rock iguana. I believe he was here looking for treasure. In addition to the notebook, he had two maps in his effects. They had something to do with the location of the treasure he was after. All the holes that had been dug at Spanish Camp were part of his search. They are marked on one of the maps. I think someone killed him because he was getting close to finding whatever he was after, the same person who needed the notebook to learn what Kelliher had come upon to lead him to Spanish Camp after ranging all over Anegada for the last five years."

"Wait a minute, Constable. You mean treasure as in pirate treasure? As in buried chests filled with gold doubloons and pieces of eight? As in yo-ho-ho and a bottle of rum?" The DC was incredulous, as if I had said Kelliher was digging up leprechaun pots of gold he had pinpointed at the ends of rainbows.

"Yes, sir," I said, so confident of my answer that I had to look down at my feet and toe the sand.

"Well, that explains everything, doesn't it, Inspector Stoutt?" The DC spoke to Rollie but never took his eyes off me.

Rollie said nothing, glancing side to side for an available rock to crawl under.

A veil of sad disdain fell across the DC's brown eyes. "Let's suppose your pirate-treasure theory allows us to disregard the involvement of a known drug user in both incidents. It does not explain why Kelliher, or whoever he was, would conceal his identity for the purpose of conducting an activity that is perfectly legal in the Virgin Islands. It does not explain why he would return every year, with no apparent success, and without giving up, when we know the average treasure hunter exhausts his theories and enthusiasm in about a month. And it does nothing to explain who would want to put a bullet between his eyes, or why."

Deputy Commissioner Lane assumed a pedagogical manner. "If, however, Paul Kelliher and Anthony Wedderburn were involved in the movement of narcotics through the BVI, with Anegada as a transit point, one can see why Kelliher would want to conceal his identity and purpose. One can understand why it would be convenient for him to return every year for a shipping season, if you will. One can see why it would be good business to have a permanent associate who is a belonger like Anthony Wedderburn to mind the store when Kelliher returned to the US. One can even understand that the transshipment of large quantities of drugs would involve equally large quantities of money, which in turn might cause a person or persons to be motivated to unsavory acts of violence to obtain the drugs or money, such as shooting someone between the eyes."

"It does not explain why he would dig all those holes, or mark their locations on a map," I said, expending my last shred of persistence.

"Actually, it explains it perfectly," the DC said. "There is a real-life example, from just last month. The Joint Interagency Task Force South found a hundred kilos of cocaine buried in a deserted area just inland from a beach in Barbados. There were dozens of holes in the area, freshly filled in, but only one with the cocaine. The others were empty, designed to mislead the curious or any potential buyers who thought they would just dig up the goods without paying. When the seller was given the money for the buy, he gave a map to the buyer showing the correct place to dig. The buyer waited with the seller while his cronies confirmed the drugs were there. The deal would have been perfect but for an informant tipping off the JITFS."

The DC concluded his lecture with a paternal pat on my shoulder. I deflated completely, my body language acknowledging the correctness of his line of reasoning though I was unable to verbalize agreement. The DC was right. I was an amateur, a special constable, not a real RVIPF officer, and had shown it by chasing some pirate-treasure fantasy to account for a crime no more glamorous than a drug deal gone bad. I still could not believe Anthony was a part of it, but deciphering the notebook probably would not have yielded the clues I had hoped. The notebook was gone now, anyway.

DC Lane deployed his forces. Rollie was sent into the church to dust for fingerprints and comb for other forensic evidence. The quartet of police officers dispersed to the four corners of The Settlement, asking questions and showing the flag. The DC marched the two hundred yards to the police station, making it his operations center. I was placed on guard at the church door, to bar the curious from entering and, more probably, to prevent me from befouling the investigation.

As the noon hour approached, Rollie emerged from inside the church. "Nothing," he volunteered. "No prints on the pieces of coral used to strike the victim. On the other hand, there must be a thousand prints on the door, table, pews, altar, everything. I'll bet if I fingerprinted everyone on Anegada, I would have a complete collection of matching prints inside this church."

I nodded in agreement.

Rollie released the crime scene to Pastor Lloyd, who responded with his thanks, an inquiry as to the best way to remove bloodstains, and a brief prayer for De Rasta.

Rollie and I drifted back to the police station, lugging his equipment cases. On arriving, we learned that the officers the DC had sent to canvass The Settlement had fared no better than Rollie. It was not that the citizens of The Settlement were not forthcoming; the novelty of a strange police officer knocking on the door was cause for plenty of excitement. The spit-and-polish boys from Road Town all got an earful but in the end no one had heard or seen anything unusual.

DC Lane seemed to take the absence of useful evidence in stride. As his next-to-last act before leaving, he placed a call to Peebles Hospital. The report on Anthony was grim. Diagnosed with a skull fracture, he remained in a coma, hooked up to the hospital's sole ventilator. Whether he would live would probably be known within the next twenty-four to forty-eight hours. If he survived that long, and could be weaned off the ventilator, the extent of the injury to his brain could be determined when the swelling caused by the blow subsided.

Hanging up the phone, the final act of the DC was to shoo Rollie and the four officers outside. When they had gone, he turned to me.

"How can these things happen in a place as small as Anegada without your knowledge?" The DC might as well have asked me why I was not a better policeman. Or why I was a corrupt policeman, if drug money was involved as he suspected.

"I don't know." It was the truth, and it cut me to the quick to say it.

The DC saw the effect of his question and the answer I was forced to give. The hard brown eyes softened perceptibly.

"Try not to devote your time to treasure maps and coded notebooks. You are the eyes and ears of the RVIPF here; keep your eyes and ears open. Call Inspector Stoutt if you learn any useful information." He placed an emphasis on "useful."

If I was to keep my eyes and ears open, I was back on the case. Or cases.

The DC stood. I stood, and came to attention for some reason.

"At ease," he grunted, and walked out the door.

Chapter Fifteen

At midafternoon on the day of Anthony Wedderburn's beating, I leaned back in the straight chair that served as my desk chair and exhaled, a deep, long, slow breath that I hoped would clear the cobwebs from my head. It had been an hour since I had taken Inspector Stoutt, Deputy Commissioner Lane, and the contingent of police officers back to the government dock for their return trip to Road Town.

The exhalation did the trick. My head cleared like a weekend drinker's on a Wednesday morning. I saw that the police work was all completed on Anthony's assault. Rollie had the forensic evidence, which would turn into nothing after he had worried over it for a few days. The four officers had spoken not only to potential witnesses but to every man, woman, and child in The Settlement. There was no physical evidence to gather and no further interviews to conduct. I was again, for all practical purposes, useless.

I tried to conjure a course of action by close examination of the dust on my desktop. No success, so I shifted my efforts to a flake of peeling paint on the opposite wall. Still depressingly useless.

Believing movement was better than ossifying at the police station, I headed out on patrol. Traveling in reverse of my usual route, it was only when I turned in the drive at Frangipani House that I realized I had not gone on patrol at all. A wretched addict, I had gone for a fix of the drug that had controlled me for these recent months.

I found Cat on a chaise beside the pool, sunning, a lithe animal, sleek and feral. She wore a white bandeau bikini, oversized sunglasses, and a white Panama hat. A bottle of Cruzan rum and a squat glass, frosted with condensation, sat on a low table beside the chaise. She turned toward me, eyes anonymous behind the dark lenses. I knelt beside her. There were beads of perspiration on her chest and flat stomach. I leaned in to taste their salt-sweet heat and I was falling, falling again, into her body and away from myself, lost and not caring, sick with need and surrender.

It was an hour before the first words were spoken. By then we floated motionless in the pool, exhausted, expended.

"I was getting lonesome, lover. Thought I might see you earlier in the day," Cat chided.

"Someone attacked Anthony Wedderburn. Clubbed him with a branch of coral inside the Methodist church. He may not live." I went on to describe the events of the day.

When I finished, she said, "Do you have any idea who did it?"

"No one seems to have seen or heard anything."

"Did they find fingerprints?"

"No. Or, rather, they found too many, from lots of different people. No way to pick out the attacker's prints from all the others in the church."

"Did they get any prints from the coral?"

"Not the pieces that were left. It looks like whoever did it took the part of the coral branch they held on to with them to dispose of later."

"How do they know no one saw or heard anything?"

I explained about the canvassing of The Settlement by DC Lane's police officers.

"Why would anyone want to do that to De Rasta?" Cat continued.

"I thought it was because of the work he was doing deciphering Kelliher's notebook. It was taken, as well as all De Rasta's working papers. Deputy Commissioner Lane thinks it's more likely tied in with the drug trade, and that Paul Kelliher's murder and the assault on Anthony are related to their involvement in trafficking. That may make some sense, but I don't like to think that about Anthony."

"Wouldn't that be a pretty logical conclusion given the way De Rasta spends most of his time stoned?" Cat was piling on with the DC and I had to agree.

"I guess so," I said reluctantly.

Cat pursued the topic. "So what are they going to do next to try to solve this?"

"Rollie Stoutt will probably take his hundreds of fingerprints and see if he gets a match with any in his database.

I doubt it, since the data is only for the BVI and we would know if there was a stranger on the island. I suppose someone could have come in the dead of night and left again before dawn without being seen, but they would have had to navigate the Horseshoe Reef in the dark and that needs local knowledge. Even an experienced boatman from Tortola wouldn't chance it in the dark."

I continued, "If Anthony lives, I'm sure he will be interviewed and he may be able to identify his attacker. If he lives. And I'm supposed to keep my eyes and ears open."

"For what?"

"I guess I'll know when I see or hear it."

"That doesn't sound like much of a plan. What if Anthony doesn't live? There doesn't seem to be much hope of solving this unless he comes out of his coma."

"Realistically, there may not be, but an unexpected break is always possible." It sounded less than hopeful as the words passed my lips.

"Will you let me know? About Anthony, I mean, let me know about his condition?" Cat's interest in the well-being of De White Rasta was mildly surprising.

"I didn't know you cared."

"He's your friend, isn't he?"

The thought had never occurred to me. "I guess he is my friend."

"Then that makes his well-being important to me," Cat said with a sincerity usually reserved for declarations of love or innocence. I was touched.

"And I hope that what the deputy commissioner thinks about him being involved in drug trafficking isn't true, for your sake as well as his," she continued.

"What do you mean, for my sake?"

"Think about it, Teddy. How would it look for you, the only police and customs official on Anegada, to have a friend who is a drug trafficker?"

"But there is no drug trafficking on Anegada. Anthony can't be a drug trafficker." I wanted it to be true but the seed planted by the DC had taken root and grown into dark doubt.

"I am just saying, lover, be careful. People are not always what they seem." Cat curled against me, turned her green eyes to mine and then down. Her hand moved along the inside of my thigh.

End of conversation.

Chapter Sixteen

In the past, I never devoted much thought to what it took to be a good policeman. Now I understood that, just as an unused machine rusts until it binds and becomes a useless mass of metal, a policeman in a place that lacks crime stops thinking like a policeman. The rituals of police work become a kind of Kabuki theater, elaborate and stylized, but devoid of content. The uniform is worn, but without pride. The patrols are completed, but without vigilance. The policeman appears to be there but in actuality has ceased to be a policeman.

These were my happy thoughts as I stared out at the glass-blue waters of Walkover Set Bay. A quarter mile west of the picturesque crescent of Cow Wreck Bay, it is a lonely place, nondescript and hard to reach, even for Anegada. Why forgo the charms and amenities of Cow Wreck for the narrow, achromatic coral detritus that comprises the beach at Walkover

Set? There is no good reason; as a result, it is the most deserted of all the island's beaches and bays. Ever since I was a small child, Walkover Set Bay is where I have gone to be alone and do my deepest thinking.

It had only been twenty-four hours since I had carried Anthony Wedderburn, to all appearances lifeless, from the Methodist church. It had only been twelve hours since I had pushed my exhausted body away from Cat Wells and walked out the front door of Frangipani House with an exhausted spirit. The last hour had been spent watching the molten orb of the sun rise from the Anegada Trench, thinking about what DC Lane had said and realizing what a poor policeman I was. It had taken two savage crimes to awaken me to the desecration of my beloved Anegada, to open my eyes to the ugly probability that it had become a drug-trafficking waypoint while in my care.

If there was a trafficking connection between Paul Kelliher and Anthony Wedderburn, there had to be another person or persons on Anegada who had been involved in the murder and assault. I decided to rule out Anthony as the murderer. He would not have reported the body if he had done the crime, and no one would have been the wiser. So who associated with both Kelliher and De Rasta? Literally everyone on Anegada knew Anthony from his years on the island.

The same could not be said of Paul Kelliher, who had kept to himself. People knew of him but did not interact with him except at the Cow Wreck Beach Bar. And even there only Belle Lloyd could claim to know him well, if anyone could.

She also knew De White Rasta, of course. She occasionally allowed him to sleep in the bar, provided he was out early before customers arrived. And then there was her reaction to me a few days ago, ordering me out of her place.

A return visit with Belle seemed like a good idea, but before the Land Rover could be reversed and turned toward Cow Wreck, the abrasive voice of Pamela Pickering issued from the CB radio.

"Teddy, Teddy, pick up! It Pamela," she said, as if her distinctive shriek required identification.

"Teddy here. What is it, Pamela?" Irritation probably came through in my voice, though there was no reason to be irritated with Pamela. Perhaps the mere fact she was Pamela was reason enough.

"Teddy, my cousin Constance—you remember my cousin Constance, don't you, from St. Croix?"

Now I was justified in my irritation. "Yes, Pamela."

"My cousin Constance, she's comin' to visit me today an' she took the *Bomba Charger* over an' when she was gettin' off at the government dock she see the *St. Ursula* come in beside the *Charger* at the dock and it full of mens with big guns and she say they all call for two taxis to pick them up at the dock an' bring them here, right here to the administration building, an' they be here any minute because the two taxis pass her on the road in, an' I thought you need to know right away an' you need to be here when them mens come an' I got to tell you I am a little frightened of guns if they bringin' guns an' will you come right over?"

"I will come as fast as I can, Pamela," I interrupted. "I'm on my way from Walkover Set Bay."

"Walkover Set, what you doin' way over there? Them mens be here with those guns any second." Pamela moved quickly to hysteria.

"I'll be there as soon as I can. Out." And I did go as fast as the washboard road permitted, banging my head against the car roof twice before hitting the smooth pavement at the edge of The Settlement. Thirty seconds later I wheeled into the gateway of the administration building.

The dusty yard of the administration building had taken on the appearance of a low-budget-film portrayal of a banana republic revolution. Half a dozen shabby characters loitered near the building or in the shade of a tall loblolly tree off to the corner of the parking area.

There were two lounging on the steps, dressed in camouflage fatigues, tan desert boots, and boonie hats, pulled low. A squat man wearing black felony flyers, calf-length black board shorts, a pound of gold chain, and a black ball cap ghettoed at a right angle to his face leaned against the trunk of the loblolly. He was receiving a lecture from a dude sporting the biggest Afro I had seen since the seventies, white pants, pastel T-shirt, and cream jacket rolled at the sleeves—full *Miami Vice* save for his bare feet.

On the opposite side of the tree, an emaciated man with a midnight-black complexion was a Jamaican tourism advertising campaign gone awry, wearing a black, green, and yellow tie-dyed T-shirt and shorts, with a knit tam of the same colors cocked to the side of his head. He looked on while a mustached man in khaki pants and shirt, black beret, and aviator sunglasses spoke menacingly to Pamela Pickering, punctuating his words with a finger jabbed at her face.

The spectacle might have been comical but for the armament the men carried. Each of the Camo Boys rested an AR-15 on his knees. Board Shorts had a beautifully chromed Mossberg riot gun slung barrel-down across his back. Miami Vice's gestures revealed a Colt 1911 in a shoulder holster beneath his jacket. Jamaica Man had a Dirty Harry–sized revolver in a low holster on his hip. Over his shoulder, Black Beret carried a mean little HK MP5 on a tactical web sling. Each of the six wore a gold badge clipped to his belt or dangling on a chain from his neck.

Pamela spotted me and called out, "Teddy, these men want to go in your office without you an' I told 'em—"

"I told you to shut up, *chica*!" Black Beret snarled. He was the only person I ever saw succeed in cutting Pamela Pickering off in midsentence.

I stepped from the RVIPF Land Rover at the same time a seventh figure emerged from the front door of the police station. Of average height with a shaved head, he wore a black T-shirt with "DEA" in white letters on the front and back, and camo pants tucked into black leather combat boots. Holstered butt-forward on his left hip was an honest-to-God Colt Peacemaker with a white bone handle.

The appearance of the Seventh Man caused an immediate reaction from the others. The Camo Boys jumped up and fell in step behind him, rifles at port arms. Board Shorts went from his relaxed lean on the loblolly to erect attention. Miami Vice stopped midlecture and coolly shifted to face the Seventh Man. Jamaica Man and Black Beret both turned their attention from Pamela to the man striding toward me.

Seven spoke to Black Beret without changing course. "You treat that woman with respect, Chavez, or I'll come over there and kick your ass."

Chavez began to puff with macho indignation, thought better of it, and muttered, "*Sí, señor.*"

"What's that, Chavez? Speak up and speak English, this ain't Santo Domingo," Seven said evenly.

Chavez reddened from ear to ear and shouted, "Yes, sir!"

His little conversation with Chavez had carried Seven to a spot immediately in front of me. He studied me for a moment with flat black eyes. They were predator eyes, the eyes of a shark, without a shred of humanity in them.

"You must be Creque. I'm Agent Rosenblum, US DEA, on loan to Joint Interagency Task Force South. I'm here to clean up your crappy little island."

If that was supposed to be an introduction, it didn't generate a warm welcome to Anegada for Agent Rosenblum from me. For a moment, I was too confounded to speak.

"I need to see your office files. Now." Agent Rosenblum obviously did not subscribe to the homily that more flies are caught with honey than vinegar.

"On whose authority?" I said, regaining enough presence of mind to ask the question.

"On my authority, Shirley, which is all the authority I need. Let's get moving."

The Camo Boys leaned forward a bit, expecting action.

"I cannot let you see RVIPF records without my supervisor's authorization."

"You mean Deputy Commissioner Lane? Fine, Shirley, you call him right up. He's the one who invited me and my men to this godforsaken rock," Rosenblum sneered.

The Camo Boys trailed loosely behind me as I went inside the police station, just close enough to make me feel I was under guard without anyone's actually saying so. When I entered my office and began to close the door, one of them placed a hand on it and shook his head. Both then stepped outside the door frame, no doubt listening through the opening.

DC Lane was on the line quickly, greeting me with "I guess the officers from JITFS have arrived."

"Unannounced. With an arsenal. They have all but taken over the police station. They say they are here because you asked them to come. Why was I not told they were coming?" I raged inside, but hearing my own voice, I realized I sounded more hurt than angry.

"Take it easy, Special Constable. You have to understand how the JITFS works. They usually arrive unannounced to all but the highest command structure of the local police agency. They bring in overwhelming force and are heavily armed because they can never be certain what they are walking into and any backup they may need is a long distance away. Their methods are unorthodox but they get results. They have made a huge impact on narcotics trafficking in the eastern Caribbean. And Agent Rosenblum has one of the best arrest records in JITFS."

"I'll say their methods are unorthodox," I said, trying to muster some of the anger I felt into my inflection. "They seem to treat everyone as a criminal suspect, including the administrator and me."

"Where drug trafficking reaches some of the most isolated islands, local authorities are often complicit." The deputy commissioner stopped speaking, his words hanging in the air, discomforting as an ex-wife in the front row at a second-marriage wedding ceremony.

"Do you think I am involved in drug trafficking?" My anger was now palpable.

"No one said that. And I do not want to think that, either," the DC said soothingly. "This is just something that had to be done. So cooperate with Agent Rosenblum and his men. They are to have full access to any records and information. Provide them with transportation. Answer their questions. They may help uncover the source of Anegada's crime problem."

I had my answer and my orders but I could not let the DC go without a final question. "Did you call them in?"

"The commissioner, the premier, and the governor made the decision to call in the task force because of the suspicion that the recent crimes on Anegada had their genesis in drug trafficking." The deputy commissioner's answer had an air of press conference formality. "Now, Special Constable, you have your orders. Do not keep your guests waiting."

"Yes, sir. Guests." Rude guests with guns who think I turn a blind eye to drug trafficking. "Very well, sir."

One of the Camo Boys must have retrieved Agent Rosenblum when he sensed the conversation was ending. The flat black eyes stared at me from the doorway when I turned away from the phone.

"Cleared things up with the home office, Shirley? Good, now where are your reports on the murder and the assault?"

"My name is not Shirley. It is Special Constable Creque to you."

"All right, Special Constable Creque, where are the damn reports?" Rosenblum delivered this question in the same tone he had used with Black Beret Chavez a few minutes before.

"I have no written reports on either incident. My reports were verbal to Deputy Commissioner Lane and Inspector Stoutt. I assume Inspector Stoutt prepared written reports as he is the investigating officer assigned to the cases."

"Do you have any field notes, witness statements, or random thoughts jotted on the back of cocktail napkins, Special Constable?"

"No."

"You can write, can't you?"

"Yes."

"Well, do you have any written reports in connection with any of your police work here, Special Constable Creque?" Agent Rosenblum spat the title and name out like he was expelling a vile-tasting insect that had flown into his mouth.

"I have my quarterly crime data reports to Deputy Commissioner Lane."

"Where?"

I gestured to the gray steel file cabinet in the corner. "Top drawer."

"Okay, Special Constable Creque, take a walk, but don't go far. I'll call you if I need anything," Rosenblum said, pulling open the drawer of the file cabinet.

Chapter Seventeen

Pamela Pickering stood shaking and crying silently in the black shade of the loblolly. Rosenblum's men had all moved away from her, loitering near the door to listen to Rosenblum belittle me rather than watching her sniffle. They parted like a pack of hungry curs as I emerged, barely giving room for me to pass. I walked to Pamela and put my arm around her shoulder to comfort her. It was the first time I could remember feeling anything toward her other than irritation. I guess Agent Rosenblum just brought out the best in people.

Two seconds later one of the Camo Boys popped out the door and said, "Chief wants to see all of us inside except Chavez. Chavez, you're supposed to post up here and keep our hosts company."

"*Tengo todos los trabajos de mierda*," Chavez griped.

"Maybe you wouldn't always get the shitty jobs if you didn't have a shitty attitude, mon," laughed Jamaica Man.

Chavez glared the glare of the rightfully accused convinced of his own blameless innocence. While his compatriots filed inside, he spat on the ground and settled a malevolent eye on Pamela and me. Pamela whimpered and sank down to her knees. I stood next to where she knelt on the hard stone, wondering how these people could call themselves policemen.

After half an hour, Jamaica Man reappeared in the doorway and beckoned me inside with a curt nod of his bushy Afro. I was ushered into my own office to find Agent Rosenblum sitting behind my desk, the thin file of my quarterly crime reports open before him.

"You are one helluva lawman, Special Constable Creque. Twenty years of reports to the boss showing no crime on this shitbox. You must be frigging Dirty Harry, John Wayne, and Superman all rolled into one."

"Anegada is a quiet place, Agent Rosenblum." You nasty, sarcastic asshole, I wanted to say, but didn't. Best to take his guff, play it straight, and not give him a reason to be more hostile to me than he already was. As if it were possible for him to be more hostile.

"I'll tell you what I think, Special Constable Creque. I think no place, no matter how quiet, how wonderful, how just-wiped-its-ass-with-a-silk-handkerchief clean it is, has no crime for twenty years. I think there are no reports of crime because if there was crime there might be a real cop posted out here in your barnyard paradise. I think a quiet place without a lot of scrutiny and a friendly local cop is just what a drug-trafficking operation needs. I think you are a dirty little cop, Special Constable Creque, except you aren't enough of a cop to be called a cop. No, come to think of it, you are just dirty." Rosenblum smiled sweetly. "That is what I think."

Play it straight. Don't lose your temper. The mantra of those words resonated inside my head, finally defeating the anger that rose in my chest. "While every island in your world is a crime-ridden drug haven, and every local policeman is corrupt, that isn't true of Anegada or of me."

"Well, that certainly persuades me, Special Constable Creque. I'll just put those impure thoughts right out of my mind," Rosenblum said, waiting for me to rise to the bait.

I just stared at him, and he unflinchingly stared back, fixing his soulless eyes on me. We remained locked on each other that way for what seemed like an hour, and was probably a minute, before Agent Rosenblum growled, "Fine. Take me to where this Kelliher's body was found."

An hour later I found myself marching along the tide line south of Flash of Beauty, matched stride for stride by a silent Agent Rosenblum. The two Camo Boys trailed behind like a pair of faithful Labradors. The others in Agent Rosenblum's force had been assigned to canvass The Settlement for clues and suspicious persons. I got the feeling that the novelty of having armed men trooping through the streets and knocking on doors might begin to wear thin for the folks in town.

When we crested the dune at Spanish Camp, I could see that Anegada had already begun to erase the evidence of Paul Kelliher's presence and his misfortune there. The once-yellow

POLICE LINE tape, torn and fluttering in several places where cattle had broken through, had faded to a buttery beige. Hoof prints crisscrossed the area that had once been bounded by the tape. Sun, wind, and rain had smoothed the edges of all the human footprints, like so many worn moon craters in miniature. The backpacker tent, which had housed Kelliher in life and his corpse in death, had come unpegged on one side and collapsed into a puddle of green plastic. The whole place had a ghost-town feel, abandoned and forlorn. Perhaps De White Rasta was right about its harboring duppies, after all.

Agent Rosenblum surveyed the area from the top of the barrier dune and then barked an order to the Camo Boys. "Swab the tent, inside and out."

The Camo Boys made for the tent, pulling packets of what looked like moist towelettes, and latex gloves, from the thigh pockets of their fatigue pants as they went. Snapping on the gloves, they tore open the packets, wiped down the tent zipper and entrance, and looked closely at the wipes. One of them glanced to Agent Rosenblum and gave a negative shake of his head. They proceeded to turn the tent inside out, tear open more wipes, and set to work on the interior.

Rosenblum ambled over to an open excavation, probably Kelliher's last, because a shovel rested on the sand beside it. Rosenblum called, and one of the Boys ran over and swabbed the shovel blade and handle. Both officers examined the towelette with crystal-ball intensity, again turning away disappointed.

Rosenblum grabbed the shovel, hopped to the bottom of the

hole, and probed. The shovel blade scraped along the limestone just below the surface of the sand at the base of the hole. After a few pokes at the sides of the excavation, Rosenblum climbed out and went on to the next. And the next. And the next, all receiving the same treatment, all yielding nothing of interest.

The Camo Boys, their scrutiny of the tent completed, each took a tent pole and began to check the excavations not already tested, working outward from the ones nearest the tent. This went on wordlessly for two hours, until all the excavations had been examined. I was relegated to watching, again, inside the tattered tape this time, but even more of an exile from the search than when the deputy commissioner sent me to watch from the crest of the dune. No longer merely incompetent, I was now an object of suspicion. Agent Rosenblum certainly would not have had me accompany him if he had believed he could find the crime scene on his own.

After the last excavation was searched, Rosenblum looked directly at me and said, “Waste of my time.”

He started east up the dune, toward the sea, the Camo Boys at heel. I climbed the dune a dozen yards behind, wishing I had never seen this place.

Sarcasm, in small doses and with correct timing, used to be my favorite brand of humor. Sarcasm toward a subordinate, again timely and in small doses, struck me as an effective management tool. Sarcasm as the primary means of communicating with those who work at your direction cannot be anything but demeaning and ineffective. This point seemed to be lost on Agent Rosenblum as he addressed his men assembled in the shade of the loblolly outside the administration building.

"So all you ladies banged down every outhouse door in this miserable shithole; strolled to the airport; lollygagged your way out to catch some rays on the government dock; turned over every rock, stick, gum wrapper, and used condom beside these cow paths they call roads; and got nothing? No midnight flights landing at the airport, no strange boats on the beach at dawn, no lights offshore, no rumors, no gossip, no local dolla boys with lots of new bling, no strange noises, no UFOs, no Bigfoot sightings? Shit, girls, I could get better results sitting in my crib, kicking back with a Red Stripe and watching the Yankees on the big screen. And save the DEA your princely salaries in the process. Nothing?"

Rosenblum scanned each face in the little knot of men and shook his head in exasperation. Most of his band just looked at the ground. Miami Vice was the picture of resigned boredom. Only Chavez puffed up and demanded, "What did you get, sir?" The "sir" matched the sardonic lilt of Rosenblum's speech.

Fixing his stygian eyes on Chavez, Rosenblum whispered, "Nothing."

Miami Vice barely suppressed a titter.

"Get your gear and mount up," Rosenblum roared.

Agent Rosenblum radiated angry frustration during the silent ride to government dock. As his men loaded onto the *St. Ursula*, he turned to me and spat, "I'm not done with you, Shirley, not you or this cesspool you call home. I know in my bones that you're dirty, and I'll be back."

"You and your men are most welcome to return to our fair island anytime, Agent Rosenblum." I smiled a warm, friendly, sarcastic smile, all teeth and rube sincerity. It felt good.

Chapter Eighteen

The good feeling occasioned by the departure of Agent Rosenblum and his merry men lasted almost until the *St. Ursula* was out of sight. Almost, but not quite. The boat was still a hazy speck against the corpulent backdrop of Virgin Gorda when the euphoria of no longer dealing with suspicion and sarcasm was replaced by the realization that the investigation of Paul Kelliher's murder and the assault on Anthony Wedderburn was back at first inning again.

Deciding it best to pick up where I had left off hours before, I turned the Land Rover toward Cow Wreck Bay for a visit with Belle Lloyd. On the way, I reached Icilda on the CB radio and explained that police business would keep me out past dinner. Her reaction was neither surprise nor disappointment. The kids would stay with friends, as she was off to yet another committee meeting at the Methodist church. I was to find dinner where I could. The entire thirty-second exchange between us took place with all the ardor of two people discussing who would get up and put out the cat. I realize now writing this that our conversations had been following this pattern for years.

The fat red sun was lowering into the sea by the time I turned down the path to Cow Wreck Bay. A rain squall darkened the sky over the Anegada Trench but promised no rain for the shore. The trade wind from the southeast passed over the island, cooling before it reached Cow Wreck Bay, making the sunset air pleasant.

It was Sunday night and, with the Saturday-to-Saturday bareboaters all returned to Tortola, a quiet evening at the Cow Wreck Beach Bar and Grill. "Quiet" is an understatement. There was probably more going on in the little cemetery beside the Methodist church. There were no patrons to be seen as I walked under the palm-thatch roof. The only sign of life was a trio of candle lamps burning at each end of the bar, anticipating the coming darkness.

I caught sight of Belle, skirt hiked up and knee-deep in the bay, peering down into her lobster pen. With a fluid motion, she reached in and plucked a lobster out by its two long antennae. The creature thrashed its tail a couple times and hung motionless, defeated and awaiting its fate.

Belle slogged a few steps toward shore before she spotted me. "The first words out of your mouth better be an apology, Teddy Creque," she called. "Otherwise, you can just turn right around and go back the way you came."

"I do apologize, Belle. I had no reason to treat you the way I did. I'm sorry. Our friendship is important to me and I hope you can forgive me for my foolishness." I was truly contrite.

"In that case, I'm grillin' one of these bugs for dinner. If you want to join me, I got a six-pounder we can share in the pen. I'll never sell it to a tourist. It's way too big for one person."

"I would love that, Belle."

Belle picked up her skirt to wade back to the lobster pen. "Light the fire then," she said, gesturing toward a pile of torchwood sticks outside the bar.

I scooped a shallow pit in the sand, tossed in an armload of sticks, touched a match to them, and had a roaring fire going in three minutes. Meanwhile, Belle had replaced the chicken lobster she had selected with a hefty specimen that flipped and jerked at the end of her arm as if it knew what was to befall it.

Stepping up to a plank she kept outside the bar lean-to, she slapped the lobster down, laid a rusty machete lengthwise down its carapace, and struck the blade with three well-placed blows of an equally rusty hammer. Bits of lobster shell and entrails showered in all directions. Though it was divided longitudinally in half, the lobster continued to kick for a few seconds before falling motionless.

Torchwood has its name because it burns bright, hot, and fast. By the time Belle placed a metal grate on the four coral chunks I had arranged at the corners of the fire, the torchwood had reduced to a glowing bed of embers. The two portions of the unfortunate lobster went on the grate immediately, cut-side down. The succulent meat sizzled and hissed, smelling of the sea. After a few minutes, Belle turned the halves with a mangrove stick. When the lobster shell turned red, we pulled it off the fire, waiting a few moments for it to cool. Then, in the Anegadian tradition, we tore out the meat with our bare hands, dunking it in bowls of Belle's vinegary Scotch bonnet pepper sauce before popping the sweet-hot-smoky morsels in our mouths. We quenched the fire of the pepper sauce with bottles of Heineken as we watched the last light of the sunset fade off Cow Wreck Low Point.

Belle idly stirred the coals of the fire with the mangrove stick. "Lawrence Vanterpool was out here today. He said De White Rasta had been beat, beat right in the Methodist church, and is nearly dead. What is happening to this place, Teddy?"

"I don't know, Belle. Maybe the world is catching up to us, or we're finally catching up to it."

Belle sighed. "It seems like the peace has gone out of our lives. Like the innocence has left this place and something ugly has stepped into its shoes."

We both fell silent, in thought, the only sound the sweep of the low surf.

"I always liked De White Rasta. Always gentle and happy, even when he came in here high as a kite," Belle said wistfully. "Which is to say every time he came in here. Do you have any idea who did it?"

"No, Belle, no suspects. I have reason to believe the assault on De Rasta is connected to Professor Kelliher's murder, that the same person or persons may be responsible for both crimes. Are you hearing anything from people?"

"Only a bunch of questions. No information that would help. Why would someone want to hurt either of them?"

"The police on Tortola think it has something to do with drug trafficking." I let the statement hang in the lowering darkness.

"I don't see either of them involved in something like that, Teddy. Whenever the professor was around, he kept to himself. He never seemed to speak to anyone but me. If he was trafficking, wouldn't he make contact with others?"

"Did you ever see him speaking with De Rasta?"

"Never. In fact, there was a time or two when they were both here, at the bar, for an evening, and neither spoke to the other. I don't think they really knew each other. And besides, I don't think De Rasta could get his act together enough to be involved in something like trafficking. He was always too baked to think about anything other than cadging enough food off me to satisfy his munchies."

"But, Belle, just because you didn't see anything happening here doesn't mean there weren't things going on away from here. Both Kelliher and De Rasta spent a great deal of time away in the more wild parts of the island. They could have met someone coming ashore on a deserted beach. Lord knows there are plenty of places that qualify for that description on Anegada." As I said this, my mind flashed briefly to an image of Cat reclining naked on the shore at Windlass Bight.

"Teddy, I would know if someone was sneaking in from

the sea. I would see a sail or superstructure on the horizon during daytime, or lights at night. Or I would hear an engine, or even voices. You know how sound carries over water. An' I ain't never seen or heard anything like that on this side of the island."

"What about airplane engines, Belle? I don't mean high up, but something low to the water, like the plane was trying to hide a drop?"

"Nothing. Well, once in a while I see the VI Birds helicopter come in low running down the length of the island. But that's just gotta be them taking some excitement-junkie tourist for a thrill ride."

"How often does that happen, Belle?" A tourist should want to see Anegada from high up, not rushing along close to the water.

"Been happening every week or so this winter."

"Which direction are they flying?"

"Always from west to east. I lose sight of them when they round Keel Point. Sometimes I hear them a few minutes later headed back the same way, but by then it's dark. I just figured it's some kind of a sunset sightseeing trip."

"It probably is, Belle," I said, thinking it probably was not. If there was a flight over Anegada as often as Belle said, I would expect to be notified, even if there was no landing requiring people to clear customs. There might not be a communication for a one-off sunset flight but repeated flights such as Belle described would always merit disclosure and an explanation in advance.

There was more than a hint of uneasiness in my gut when I considered who the pilot on those flights might be. I told myself there was probably a good explanation. I told myself I was becoming like Agent Rosenblum, seeing a drug conspiracy behind even the most innocent act. I told myself Cat would never get caught up in running drugs, that she was too good for that, too smart for that. I told myself these things and I did not believe them for a second.

The inner voice is one's closest confidant. When the wisdom it imparts is doubted, the world trembles with the brush of a gnat's wing and is toppled by a grain of sand. Now I felt as though I stood in a hurricane, a cascade of pink pearl granules from Cow Wreck Beach tumbling down upon me.

Thank God it was too dark for Belle to see my face. We spoke for a few minutes more, about what I cannot recall. My mind was too busy running over the information about the VI Birds helicopter's unscheduled flights along the north side and how the period of time they were occurring coincided with the time Cat and I had been involved almost to the day.

I made a distracted and hasty departure, mumbling thanks to Belle for her hospitality. Bouncing out to the intersection of the Cow Wreck Beach path with the north shore road, I turned east toward Frangipani House and a tête-à-tête with a certain helicopter pilot residing there.

Chapter Nineteen

Frangipani House was illuminated by the low glow of a handful of oil lamps placed around its pool. An Amália Rodrigues album played on the stereo, layering the melancholy and regret of fado over Anegada's night sounds. The warm air was perfumed by the scent of the house's namesake flower.

Cat stood at the edge of the flickering shadows cast by the lamps, leaning against a pillar. She was wearing a crisp white man's shirt, as a cover-up for a bathing suit, or maybe for nothing. Thinking I might not have seen her, she said, "Over here, Teddy." Her voice broke as she said the words, as if the sadness of the fado had infected her. I felt the walls within me start to crumble, felt the same old weakness return, and tried to steel myself against it.

She came to me, laid her hand lightly on my cheek, and said, "I missed you, Teddy."

"I missed you, too," I said, and it was the absolute, undeniable truth, not altered one iota by the possibility that she might be piloting drug-running flights to Anegada. Resist, resist, I told myself, even as I understood the futility of resistance. Resist, resist, even as my every sense absorbed the dark beauty, the throaty laugh, the velvet kiss, the lusty embrace, that was Cat.

"Maybe we should get reacquainted," she whispered against my neck as she pressed her body to mine. My hands wandered over her, feeling heat, softness, and sweat. I knew I would succumb again.

And then an odd thing happened. I saw a flashback of Anthony Wedderburn, just for a moment, just as I had found him in the Methodist church, broken and bloody. Except, unlike when I found him in the church, he looked at me, opened his eyes and focused intently on mine. And then the image was gone, as was the carnal need I had felt for Cat only moments before.

I released my embrace and stepped back.

"What is wrong, lover?" Cat asked with more than a trace of disappointment. "I've been needing you."

"Sorry, Cat. It's just been a really tough last couple of days."

"I'll get you a drink and you can tell me all about it." Cat transitioned from wanton seductress to motherly bartender in an instant. She disappeared into the house, returning moments later with two glasses filled with ice, a small dish containing wedges of yellow island lime, and a quart of Cruzan rum. She tossed a lime wedge in each glass and followed with a three-finger pour of the Cruzan.

Handing me a drink, she gently steered me to the chaise, guided me down, and curled in next to me. She drank deeply. I followed suit, the burn of the rum cascading to the pit of my stomach.

"Deputy Commissioner Lane sent in a group of agents from the Joint Interagency Task Force South today, without telling me in advance," I began. "It is pretty clear that he thinks the assault on Anthony Wedderburn and Paul Kelliher's murder are drug related. The JITFS agents believe I know something about what went on, and that I'm covering for, or at least turning a blind eye to, the use of Anegada as a drug transit point. The task force agent in charge, a nasty bastard named Rosenblum, essentially told me he would see me charged and convicted."

"Oh, Teddy, that's horrible," Cat said. She shuddered and stiffened against me.

I continued. "The task force agents rifled through all the police station paperwork. They took the lack of records of any crime as confirmation of the theory that I am on the take. They had me go with them to Spanish Camp and poked around there. They knocked on doors in The Settlement asking questions, probably about whether I was a crooked cop. And they got nothing from any of it."

"Because there was nothing to get," Cat chimed in.

"That's what I thought. That's what I still think. But all this talk of drug smuggling, and no other good explanation for the recent crimes, makes me wonder if drugs might be a factor.

"Take Anthony," I went on. "He gets his ganja somehow, and has for years, without anyone, including me, discovering how, or when, or from whom. He has to have some connection to a supplier. And he was beaten while deciphering a code book for me, a book that might have had information about drug trafficking in it. Maybe he had no intention of deciphering the book, or maybe he intended to mislead me about its contents."

"Maybe the book was not the reason he was beaten," Cat suggested. "Maybe he was beaten to keep him quiet. After all, the Methodist church is not exactly a secret hideout. Anyone could have seen him there and taken the book just to throw you off the track."

"If that's correct, it would still leave me nowhere with a theory for a motive. And drug smuggling would be more plausible if there were some other evidence to support it, if someone had seen or heard something unusual, a boat at sea, an after-dark beach landing, people sneaking onto the island." I had the hopeless feeling I imagined one might have before a suicidal leap from a cliff. "But I've heard nothing like that. And what about you, Cat? You fly over Anegada all the time. Have you seen anything out of the ordinary?" The leap, and I was in free fall.

"I almost always fly in from the southwest, Teddy, from St. Thomas, so I fly mostly over water. But, no, I've seen nothing unusual." The legato throb of her pulse against me betrayed no concern, a sharp contrast to my tachycardic heart.

"I need another drink," Cat said. "What about you?" And with that she was up, bustling over to the low table that held the rum, splashing more in both glasses.

She brought the drinks back, handing mine down as she stood over me. "This has gotten you all tense, lover. You need to relieve that tension. I can help you with that," she said, straddling me, the tail of her shirt sliding above a silken thigh. In a moment we were having sex, brutal, animal copulation, Cat above, all thrust and heat.

As we moved against each other, we both knew. I knew Cat had a part, some part, in the enterprise responsible for Kelliher's murder and De Rasta's beating. Cat knew her secret flights were no longer a secret to me. We silently grappled and sweated as if combatants locked in a battle for our lives. In the end, the silence was broken by our mutual outcry, but the cry was different now than in the past, wary and suppressed, and we parted without another word.

Chapter Twenty

The fresh start of a Monday morning loses some of its appeal when you awake realizing that your impression that your mistress is a drug-running killer is not just a bad dream. Add a wife surly because she has to work an unscheduled breakfast shift, a teenage daughter whining about the lack of stylish designer clothing in Tortola and the need for a thousand-mile shopping excursion to Miami to correct this injustice, and a son who announces out of the blue that he now knows the exact mechanics for making babies, courtesy of his best friend, Malvern "Mullet" Soares, and you have a roaring start to the week.

The domestic segment of the morning's difficulties was disposed of, temporarily, by the dispersal of adults to jobs and kids to school. I decided to start the workday by tackling the drug-running-killer-mistress issue, which arguably fell into the category of business, not to discount its significant domestic implications. Some quiet reflection at the police station seemed to be a good starting point.

When I arrived, the building was empty, a note taped to the door explaining that the administrator was taking a sick day. Pamela Pickering was certainly blameless for needing a mental health day after the trauma inflicted by Agent Rosenblum and his men. Her absence provided an opportunity to use the computer in her office without unnecessary and potentially embarrassing questions about why I was searching for information on VI Birds' sexy female helicopter pilot. And pecking away at Pamela's sticky computer keyboard sure beat my previous plan for the morning of staring at the peeling mustard-yellow paint on the wall while trying to come up with a way to explain my suspicions of Cat to the deputy commissioner, and the guaranteed fallout of that explanation.

As a mere special constable, I had no access to any closed police databases, either international or those of the RVIPF. I considered calling Rollie Stoutt to ask him to search those restricted sources for information on Cat but quickly discarded the idea. While I might count on his indifference to prevent any interference with my investigation, a request for him to actually do something might be a catalyst for a conversation with the DC, a can-of-worms unveiler I wished to avoid.

In the end, I opted for the public access route, and after two hours on the Web was rewarded with a shattering headache and no worthwhile information of any sort about Mary

Catherine Wells. I medicated myself with two aspirin and decided to go over the results of my search from a few days before to see if there was anything of value I had missed.

Ten minutes later I was staring at the grainy photograph of Cat and her fellow pilots from Desert Storm. Looking at the .38 Smith & Wesson holstered on her hip, I had to wonder if it was the weapon that had turned Paul Kelliher from faux biologist into crab bait. Cat spoke about the gun so affectionately in the *Houston Chronicle* article that I had to assume she would still have it. It was probably unregistered, and with the ease of gun ownership in the US, probably hidden in her apartment in St. Thomas. But I had no basis for ballistics testing of the gun even if I could access it, and no bullet or bullet fragment from Kelliher's remains to compare it with.

I reread the article hoping for something, anything, to jump out at me. Seeing again that Cat had lived on Puerto Rico, I tried to find information on the army base there and learned that the base, Fort Buchanan, had closed as an army facility in 1966. Cat would not have been born at that time. While the article said she had lived in a number of other places in her youth, any information on her in those places was not available through a search under her name.

I decided to try her father's name, hoping to obtain information on Cat through him. The first search result about Neville Wells was his obituary from the archives of the *Winfield Daily Courier* of Winfield, Kansas. The details of his years from 1941 to 1991 were compressed into one paragraph, a half century summarized in prose as austere as the Kansas plain:

Neville Wells passed away March 1, 1991, at his home in Winfield. He was born January 2, 1941, in Detroit, Michigan. A career army pilot and Vietnam veteran, Mr. Wells is survived by a daughter, Mary Catherine Wells, who is currently serving with the US Army in Operation Desert Storm. Funeral arrangements are through Swisher-Taylor & Morris Funeral Home in Winfield. Interment will be at Highland Cemetery.

No memorial or church service was mentioned. No surviving spouse or relatives other than Cat were named.

The next search result fairly popped with information about Neville Wells's military career. Chief Warrant Officer Wells was on the "Dead After Tour" name list of a veterans group, the Vietnam Helicopter Pilots Association. Clicking on his name revealed that his unit was the Sixty-Eighth Assault Helicopter Company, with which he served two tours in Vietnam, ending in 1965. His helicopter's in-country call sign, "Hamburger 5," was even noted.

A link to a site maintained by another veteran of the Sixty-Eighth AHC contained photocopied pages of the unit history written during the war, together with a wealth of photographs. CWO Wells was referred to in several portions of the unit history by his nickname, "Tree-Level Neville," a reference to his favorite tactic of flying at treetop height to avoid enemy antiaircraft fire.

There was a photograph of CWO Wells, with his flight crew, in front of their UH-1 Huey, dripping jungle and thatched hooches in the background. He carried the Smith & Wesson .38 he would later give to Cat in a shoulder holster. His name and the names of the rest of the flight crew had been typed along the bottom of the photo with a manual typewriter, the letters slightly askew.

The anonymous webmaster of the Sixty-Eighth AHC site made up for in enthusiasm what he lacked in organizational skill. The site was a mishmash of photos, histories, lists, and notices of reunions. Paging through, I stumbled on a section entitled "Post-Tour History," which detailed many of the unit members' lives after their time in Vietnam. These biographical summaries were not in alphabetical order. Some consisted of paragraph after paragraph describing later military postings, marriages, education, children's names, dates of discharge, and civilian jobs. Some contained only a name and date of death.

After flicking through this section for almost an hour, I came to the bio for Neville Wells. According to its unnamed author, CWO Wells was posted to Fort Buchanan in San Juan, Puerto Rico, after his tours in Vietnam. He was honorably discharged from the army in 1966, reenlisted in 1970, and served in Germany, Hawaii, and Japan before his second honorable discharge and retirement in 1987. The fact of retirement was the last information in the bio, Wells's death in Kansas having escaped the author's notice.

All this provided little additional information pertaining to Cat. It did serve as confirmation of her youth spent as an army brat, bouncing from post to post, although it appeared likely she was born in the gap between Neville Wells's discharge in 1966 and his reenlistment. If the *Houston Chronicle* article about Cat was accurate, her time living in Puerto Rico would have been when her father was not in the military. There did not appear to be any significance to this.

Four hours of searching had only succeeded in increasing the intensity of my headache. The ancient history I had unearthed about "Tree-Level" Neville Wells was a waste of time. I took this as further confirmation that, as a policeman, my investigative techniques left much to be desired.

I rummaged through the top drawer of Pamela Pickering's desk, searching for another dose of aspirin. Frustrated in that search as well, I leaned back in her chair with my hands over my eyes, willing them to rest in the hope that my headache would abate on its own. The warm part of the day had arrived. I dozed through the dull throb at the base of my skull, drifting through a dream of Cat in the jungles of Vietnam, Smith & Wesson in hand, haggling over a drug deal with a corrupt ARVN general.

Then the telephone began to ring in my office across the hall.

Chapter Twenty-One

I cannot remember the last time there had been an unexpected call made to my office telephone. A truly unanticipated call, not in response to an inquiry made to headquarters, not scheduled in advance, was blue-moon rare at the police station. If an Anegadian ever wanted to reach me, a CB radio is what was used. And no one who was not an Anegadian ever wanted to reach me.

Three steps and I was in my office. The ringing seemed to stop, and I stared for a second at the heavy black government-issue phone. Had I imagined the ring? Then it rang again, and I realized the ringing had not actually stopped. I had moved so quickly time seemed to slow between rings.

I snatched the dusty receiver from its cradle. "Anegada Police Station."

"Special Constable Creque, please," said the pleasant,

Midwestern American voice on the line. The connection was poor, with a bottom-of-a-barrel echo.

"This is Special Constable Creque," I said.

"Ah, Constable, this is Detective Sergeant Donovan, from the Boston PD Missing Persons Unit. We spoke last week," the voice said, the last statement half a question, almost asking if the speaker was remembered.

"Yes, Sergeant Donovan, good afternoon. What a pleasure to hear from you. To what do I owe this honor?"

Sergeant Donovan tried to be matter-of-fact, but there was a trace of professional pride coming through in his answer. "I think I've found your Paul Kelliher, or rather the person who he actually was."

"The person he actually was? You mean he was not using his real name?"

"That's right. His real name was John Ippolito. Paul Kelliher was a ghost identity he assumed."

"A ghost identity?"

"The identity of a deceased individual taken by someone to conceal their true identity, Constable," Donovan explained. "In this instance, Paul Kelliher was the deceased individual."

Sergeant Donovan launched into his explanation. "It took a few days to put this all together, but as nearly as I can confirm, the real Paul Kelliher was born in Putnam, Connecticut, in 1945, son of James and Mabel Kelliher. His father died in 1950, and shortly thereafter, Mabel moved to Boston with young Paul. She remarried in 1962 to a Boston native, a high school teacher named Charlie Abreu. Sometime later that same year, Paul obtained a Social Security number, probably because he got an after-school job and was required to have one.

"In November 1962, Charlie Abreu legally adopted Paul, who became Paul Abreu. The entire family, Charlie, Mabel, and young Paul, died in a house fire on Christmas Eve 1963. Being during the holidays and wiping out an entire family, it made all the papers in Boston. The family was buried together in Mount Hope Cemetery in Mattapan. I went there and saw the marker.

"This next part is speculation, but it's educated speculation, because I've seen a number of these cases. This kind of identity assumption happens more than the average person would expect. My speculation is that our man, sometime in the late 1990s, decided he needed another identity, for whatever reason. He visited Mount Hope Cemetery searching for headstones of males born in approximately the same year he was born. He found Paul Abreu and somehow obtained a death certificate for him. It wasn't hard to do, in the days before 9/11. A friend who works in the city registry division, or maybe a few bucks passed along with a story about putting together a family genealogy, was all it would take. From there, he checked public records, found the probate case and maybe even the adoption proceedings, and learned Paul's place of birth and birth name.

"So next he made a trip to the Putnam city clerk's office with a request for a certified copy of Paul's birth certificate.

Maybe he produced a false ID, maybe he sold a sob story to a small-town clerk, or maybe he paid a bribe, but when he left he had real ID as Paul Kelliher, in the form of a birth certificate.

"Even better, between two different states and two different surnames for Paul, no one notified the Social Security Administration of the real Paul's death. The Social Security number remained listed as active and somehow, God only knows how, our ghost got the number. He then had the golden tickets to a new identity—a name that is somewhat distinctive but with a nice common Boston Irish sound, no close relatives alive to stumble onto his use of the dead teen's name, a genuine birth certificate, and an active Social Security number. From that point forward he can easily get a driver's license, passport, and any other identification he needs or wants. He can invent a wife, family, job, and life story that he can use in a place like your British Virgin Islands with impunity because his paperwork is correct and no one has a reason to disbelieve any of it or even check it out. Until he turns up dead."

"It's amazing that someone would go to that extent to conceal his true identity unless he had something serious to hide. Did you learn any reason why he would do this?" I asked.

"No, Constable, looks like it's up to you to fill in the blanks on that."

"Just how did you connect all this to John Ippolito?" I asked.

Donovan chuckled softly. "Normally, Constable, I don't

reveal my trade secrets, not even to the folks at the BPD. A touch of mystique is great for old Sergeant Donovan's reputation with the bosses around here. But I guess I can make an exception, given your distance and my impression that you are a good guy in a tough spot."

"I appreciate that," I said, wondering how he could tell I was in a tough spot.

Donovan went on. "Your guy had his ghost identity all set up, except for one thing, the thing you need more in the United States of America than almost anything else."

"What is that?" I bit when he paused for effect. Detective Sergeant Donovan could be theatrical.

"Credit. You are nothing in twenty-first-century America without the ability to get credit. You can hardly exist without a credit card, to travel, to rent a car, to buy a plane ticket. So, I have this contact at Experian."

"What is Experian?" I asked sheepishly.

"Jesus, Constable, it must be like living in Mayberry in 1950 down there. I gotta come and visit sometime."

"You are always welcome," I said, and meant it.

"Anyway, Experian is one of the big credit reporting agencies. You can't get credit without a report from one of them, and they know more about the average American than the FBI, NSA, local cops, and their own mama will ever know.

"I had my contact at Experian run a credit report on Paul Kelliher," Donovan continued, now on a roll. "She used the Social Security number that had been issued for Paul Kelliher in Boston in 1962. Maybe not quite kosher for my contact to do, but she and I, well, we go a long way back, and I once did her a favor by marrying her and an even bigger favor by divorcing her. She tells me Paul Kelliher has a credit history a yard long. But the personal info in the report showed a different address than the one you gave me from his passport application and driver's license.

"I was so excited by the new lead that I offered to thank my contact by buying her a drink, but she declined, suggesting I do my drinking alone, like I did when we were married. With nothing better to do, I decided to take a cruise over to the credit report address, 319 D Fulton Street in the North End. Hauled my somewhat-outta-shape carcass to the apartment on the top floor of the building, a three-story walk-up; knocked on the door; and, surprise, nobody's home.

"But the busybody two doors down pokes her head out and asks me what do I want. There's one in every building in these old neighborhoods. I showed her my badge and told her I wanted to talk to the occupant. She practically wet her pants with excitement and spilled everything she knew about the guy who rented the apartment, which was a lot.

"Your man rented under the name of John Ippolito. He had lived there for about a year. Never had any visitors and kept to himself. Then he moved out about three months ago, never said a word to any of the neighbors about leaving, just there one day and gone the next. A moving company packed up all his belongings and carried them away. Unfortunately, the busybody couldn't remember the name of the moving company. But she did recall what Mr. Ippolito did for a living. He worked for an asphalt paving company, Calabria Brothers.

She remembered seeing that on the uniform shirt he wore to work each day.

"A quick visit to Calabria Brothers filled in the blanks. The receptionist was a real badge bunny, made a point of saying she always wanted to date a cop. Not much to look at, but then neither am I. I played along and in ten minutes I knew everything there was to know about John Ippolito from Calabria Brothers, plus I got her phone number.

"Ippolito ran an asphalt paving machine and, like most of the Calabria Brothers employees, was laid off each winter when it got too cold for asphalt paving. The employees would be recalled each spring when the temps rose again, but that hadn't happened yet this year, so no one had missed him at work. He was a loner, civil but not real friendly, and not known to socialize with the other employees. He told the boss he had no family and his personnel file had no emergency contact information. No one knew what he did when he was off in the winter, but the receptionist remembered he always came back with a tan.

"I showed Miss Badge Bunny the Paul Kelliher passport photo and she ID'd it as John Ippolito. The address the company had for Ippolito/Kelliher was the Fulton Street address he had already vacated. Probably left there right after his work for the season ended and headed down to your island to get himself killed.

"Anyway, Constable, that's as far as I got with it before calling you. I still don't have any lead on next of kin but I'll run some more with it, if you think it would be helpful."

"I would be grateful if you would, Sergeant."

"That's what the good citizens of Boston pay me to do. I'll call you if I get anything more. And maybe the whole ghost identity thing will help you find who killed him."

"I hope so, Sergeant. Your efforts are most appreciated. And I meant what I said about you being welcome here if you ever get down to the Caribbean."

"Pretty long odds on me making it down there on a Boston cop's salary, especially when you deduct the alimony payments. But I appreciate the invitation. And if I turn up anything else on your man, I'll be in touch, Constable." The line clicked dead.

I dropped the telephone receiver into its cradle. The dullness of the headache lingered, a thin wash of pain from the root of my eyes. The unrelenting brilliance of the Anegada midday sun blasted through the office window, adding heat and light to the throbbing. I closed the shade, put the side of my face down on the cool metal of the desktop, and willed myself to think.

Paul Kelliher was not Paul Kelliher at all, but John Ippolito. Not a biologist, but an asphalt paver. He came to Anegada year after year not to study the rock iguana, but to do what? Run drugs? Dig up the desolate interior of the island searching for treasure? You could do either without a change of identity. Why did John Ippolito become Paul Kelliher? Why couldn't he accomplish what he wanted here as John Ippolito? Who was John Ippolito?

I slipped into a state of half-sleep and heard myself mumble "John Ippolito" in the silent room.

Then I sat bolt upright.

Chapter Twenty-Two

It can't be, it can't be, it can't be, the voice inside me repeated as I bolted down the short hall to the administrator's office. It can't be, it can't be, it can't be, as I fumbled the worthless 1-2-3-etc. password from the keyboard to the screen of Pamela Pickering's computer, pulled up Google, and pounded "Vietnam Helicopter Pilots Association" into the search box. It can't be, it can't be, it can't be, as I scrolled and clicked my way to the link to the haphazard website of the Sixty-Eighth Assault Helicopter Company veterans.

But it was, right there in the gauzy photograph of the crew of Hamburger 5 taken at Vung Tau, Vietnam, in late 1965, separated from CWO Neville Wells by two intervening crew members.

"Warrant Officer John Ippolito," the old typescript said, the "J" tilted at a crazy angle and the "t" struck over a premature "o."

Peering at the man in the photo, I tried to match him with my memory of Paul Kelliher from the times I had seen him at the Cow Wreck Beach Bar and Grill. The face in the photo was younger and leaner but the eyes were intense and unmistakable, twins to the eyes of Paul Kelliher before death extinguished their light.

There was no other information on WO Ippolito on the Sixty-Eighth AHC website. A return to the VHPA "Post-Tour History" page showed he also had been assigned to Fort Buchanan in San Juan, Puerto Rico, following his tour in Vietnam. Like Neville Wells, he received his honorable discharge from the army at that posting in 1966. Unlike CWO Wells, he never reenlisted. The VHPA had no further history for him.

Other confirmation that Warrant Officer Ippolito was the John Ippolito who had stolen young Paul Kelliher's identity was easily obtained. Googling "Vietnam Veterans Index" directed me to the US National Archives. Searching in its archival databases, I quickly found the enlistment record for John Ippolito, born in Boston, Massachusetts, in 1945, single with no dependents, civilian occupation construction laborer, enlistment date June 9, 1963. Though there were enlistment records for other John Ippolitos in the database, there was only one with the correct era, geography, and age.

There was no question or doubt. The mutilated corpse found sprawled on the baking sand at Spanish Camp was that of the man who had been stationed in Vietnam and Puerto Rico with Neville Wells, father of Mary Catherine Wells. Cat Wells, my mistress.

Cold coursed through my veins, sending a tremor along my spine. The headache that had plagued me was gone, replaced by dark foreboding. I would have much preferred a return to the headache but there was no turning back. For the first time, I knew a connection existed between Cat, her father, Ippolito/Kelliher, and Anegada, a connection dating back to the late 1960s. The matter that formed and forged the connection was still a mystery but not a total mystery. Whatever it was, I knew it was worth a half century of time. I knew it was worth lies and deceit.

I knew it was worth killing and dying for.

Chapter Twenty-Three

Anegada got an early start, as recorded history in the Western Hemisphere goes. But after the visit from Chris Columbus and the buccaneer period of the sixteenth and seventeenth centuries, the island dropped off the radar screen of history, a condition from which, blessedly, it has never recovered.

Only now I needed to know about Anegada in the late 1960s, to determine if Neville Wells and John Ippolito ever came here, and why. And I needed to know what it was that would bring Wells's daughter and Ippolito, under an assumed identity, back here after over four decades.

There are no written histories of Anegada during the sixties; there was so much happening in the wide world that places like Anegada could be ignored. To learn about Anegada in the decade before my birth, I could not read about it. I had to speak with someone who had been here then.

In most places, finding someone who had been in the area forty or even fifty years before would not be difficult, but it was a tall order on Anegada. The population back then was even smaller than today, fewer than one hundred souls. The ticket to prosperity then was the same as in many of the world's rural places, a ticket away, to a big place, a big city. In the case of Anegada, the big city of choice was one of the biggest on the planet, New York, New York. Even today, there are almost five times as many people who claim Anegadian ancestry in New York as there are on Anegada itself. Those who opted not to emigrate were subject to the third-world perils of backbreaking manual labor, poor medical care, and bad nutrition, and few of that era lived beyond their fourth decade.

Fortunately, there is one old soul still on Anegada from those days, with an encyclopedic memory and a sharp eye for detail. He is part sage, part institution, and part community conscience. I am talking about my father, Sidney Creque.

Sidney Creque was born on Anegada in 1929. Though the years of his youth encompassed the period of the Great Depression and the Second World War, the isolation of the island insulated him from the effects of those events. As a young man, he survived by subsistence farming, clawing a living from the niggardly soil, watering his crops of corn and pumpkins from the same limestone sinks that had provided water to Columbus on his brief visit four and a half centuries earlier.

A dearth of marriageable women, combined with a need to market the small surplus of his crops, sent my dada regularly to St. Thomas in a boat he had constructed from driftwood and scavenged nails. The trips did little to advance his search for a wife but did cause him to acquire a taste for Cruzan rum. He began to bring bottles back on his return voyages, and learned others on Anegada had a similar taste for the distilled cane, despite the stern temperance of the local Methodist minister. Soon he was making a monthly rum run to the USVI. He gradually expanded his product line and became the only importer of goods on an island where almost everything, other than fish, flamingoes, iguanas, and sand, must be imported.

Dada had become the most prosperous businessman on Anegada when his third cousin, Lily Brathwaite, came from Barbados to visit her aunt and uncle in the summer of 1958. By then he had given up on the St. Thomas girls and was a confirmed bachelor. Dada and Madda's eyes still shine as they speak of their love at first sight when they were introduced at a church supper. They were married two months to the day after that first meeting, and immediately embarked on an effort to more densely populate the island, Madda giving birth to my nine brothers and sisters in the next nine years. I brought up the rear of the offspring parade in the fall of 1969.

As Dada and Madda grew older, they gave away bits and pieces of their Anegada enterprises to my siblings until all that remained was Creque's Gas Dock and Gas Station. While Dada had begun the operation by barging in fifty-five-gallon drums of kerosene for lamps and pumping the contents with a hand pump, the facility was now modernized. Once a month, a gasoline barge lumbered over from Tortola to fill the single steel underground tank buried in a cut in the limestone just east of the government dock. The fuel from that tank ran all the boat motors, automobiles, and generators on Anegada.

Dada dispensed his product from an electric pump beside the road, shaded by two stubby coconut palms. While awaiting customers, he passed his time in a decrepit smudge-green Chesterfield chair housed in a shed just large enough for it and a metal cash till. He opened and closed when he felt like it, but nobody seemed to mind the irregular hours, even if they came halfway across the island and found the hand-lettered CLOSED FOR THE DAY sign on the pump at noon.

It was late in the afternoon when I rolled into the single space beside the pump. The CLOSED FOR THE DAY sign was nowhere to be seen, surprising at that hour. Dada was almost always closed by five o'clock, as Madda was punctual with supper at five thirty.

I found Dada seated inside the crowded shed, head back, mouth agape, sleeping like a stone. I made a rustling shuffle of my feet outside the door and the old man popped awake, fresh as the dawn over Table Bay rock.

"What are you doing here so late, Dada?" I asked.

"No reason to go home. Your madda is at a church meeting. Cold supper for me and a cold bed until the middle of the night," he said, slyly smiling his just-between-us-men-of-the-world smile, dentures dazzling white. "Ain't nothing like a church meeting to put a woman off in the bedroom."

Too much information, Dada, I thought. "I came to see if I could get your help on a police investigation, Dada," I said, hoping to shift from the topic of his and Madda's bedroom activities before he further expanded on it.

"Of course, you can have my help, but what can a skinny old man do to help you on an investigation?" he asked, puzzled.

"Don't worry about skinny, Dada, and the old part is just what I need. I want to ask you about Anegada in the nineteen sixties, just before I was born."

"Good thing you don't want the skinny body, boy, 'cause I'm saving all of that I can for your madda," he said, leering. No wonder I have nine siblings. "What do you want to know?"

"Do you remember any men by the name of Neville Wells or John Ippolito coming to Anegada then?"

"No. Those names aren't familiar. Who are they?"

"John Ippolito is the real name of Paul Kelliher."

"The lizard scientist? That fellow who got killed out at Spanish Camp?"

"That's right." I paused, trying to think of a way to explain my interest in Neville Wells that did not bring Cat into the discussion. "And Neville Wells was an associate of his back then. Wells has been dead for a couple decades."

"Was he white, too?" Dada asked.

"No," I said. Dada's query made sense. Seeing white folks is common on Anegada nowadays. Most of the tourists who visit are white. There are even some white families, like the Soareses, who have settled here during my lifetime. But in the sixties, there was no tourism, and whites, even in Tortola, consisted mostly of government bureaucrats sent by Her Majesty to administer the then-colony. There was no reason for a white British bureaucrat to visit Anegada, an island in the hinterlands of their hinterlands posting, and they never did.

"In the early part of the sixties, the only white men here were the Americans, the ones who built and manned the tracking station on the West End." Dada gestured westward like he was describing the far side of the moon. "There was no road out there back then. They kept mostly to themselves, I guess because they didn't want to walk all the way around to The Settlement on the beach. Not that there was anything to walk to then, not a store, not a bar, not even Cardi's Pool Hall. Just the houses and the Methodist church.

"When they first built the tracking station, some of the boys took their boats there with fish they caught, hoping to sell to the Americans, but that didn't work. The Americans had dynamited a hole in the reef so they could barge in building materials. There was dynamite left over, and when they wanted fish, they would take a stick or two out to the reef, toss them in, and have all the fish they wanted for a week without paying anything. Besides, they mostly ate out of cans, disgusting stuff flown in from San Juan by helicopter."

"By helicopter?" My antenna went up.

"Yes. Well, not at first. When they were building the Quonset huts and the big dish they used to track the space shots, they barged in all their supplies. But shortly after they finished construction, a supply barge ran aground on the reef. Those boys weren't even smart enough to put the barge through the hole they had blown open. They spilled a few hundred gallons of diesel fuel and sank the barge right where the wreck still sits today.

"After that, they didn't take any chances trying to navigate the reef; everything came in by helicopter. Usually it was one flight a week from San Juan. Once the place was built, there were only a half dozen personnel manning it, so they could easily resupply by air."

"Whose helicopters did they use?" I asked, though I felt the answer was already known to me, like watching a test match between West Indies and the boys who play pickup cricket behind the school on Saturday afternoon. The outcome was certain, even before the first ball was bowled.

Dada squinted, forcing recollection. "All US military. Mostly navy but some army from the San Juan base."

"Dada, did you ever meet any of those fliers?" I held my breath after asking, hoping against hope he had.

"No. They flew in and flew out, never stayed more than the time it took them to unload. I don't think they found Anegada to be a very attractive place to spend time."

"Did they ever fly to different parts of the island, or fly around the island?"

"The first few times they came in, you would see them circle, maybe to take a look around, but after that, they went straight in and out." It sounded unlikely that one of them might have spotted something or even landed at Spanish Camp.

"How long did the flights continue?"

"Right up until the Americans moved away in 1968. They picked up and left so fast it seemed like they were gone overnight, but it actually took them a couple weeks to get everything out. There was no notice to us on Anegada, not from the Americans or from Tortola. One day in the fall of '68, an old World War II landing ship arrived and anchored about a mile off the West End. It stayed there for a few days, with small-boat shore parties coming in every morning and leaving at sunset. They dismantled the buildings and the tracking dish and on the last day brought the landing ship through the hole in the reef, got it right that time, and dropped the ramp on shore. By nightfall, they had loaded everything—buildings, equipment, and men—on the ship and they were gone. The only trace they left was the steel matting from their helipad and the angle-iron post still out on the West End."

"Did the Americans ever come back, even temporarily, after that?"

"No. Why, did someone tell you they had?"

"No, it just seemed unusual for them to take almost everything but leave the helipad."

My father settled back in his chair and sighed. "I guess it wasn't worth taking with them, even for scrap. Anyway, the Americans never used the helipad again. The only ones who used it after that were Nigel Brooks's men."

I felt the hairs rise on the back of my neck on hearing that name.

Chapter Twenty-Four

The mention of Nigel Brooks always draws a strong reaction from any Anegadian, even those born long after his departure. He was part charismatic preacher, part flimflam man, and Brooks's reputation is second only to Mephistopheles's in the minds of the good people of the BVI. But that was not always the case.

The story is well-known in our tiny country. It began when Brooks materialized from out of nowhere in 1966. One fall day he simply appeared at the customs house in Road Town, bringing with him an affected aristocratic accent; a statuesque blonde whom he introduced to all as his wife, Cybil; and a banker's draft on the Bank of England for two hundred thousand pounds. Only after scandal reared its ugly head would it be learned that the accent covered a Cockney burr, and that the dazzling Cybil had enjoyed a prior life as a high-priced escort catering to a clientele with an affinity for whips, rubber, and leather.

The Bank of England draft, as it turned out, was real, although the source of the funds was never ascertained. But in midsixties Road Town, the deposit of the draft into the newly opened branch of Barclays bank was a secret the branch employees were unable to keep. And Brooks himself was less than discreet about the what-was-then-huge sum of money he had brought into the colony. Soon everyone in the BVI knew of Nigel Brooks's vast wealth and took the opportunity to embellish on what they knew when describing it to others.

Nigel and Cybil took up residence in the honeymoon suite of the venerable Fort Burt Hotel. A month after their arrival, a freighter originating in Southampton offloaded two crates consigned to Brooks at Road Harbour. The smaller contained the latest London fashions for Cybil and Savile Row's tropical equivalent for Nigel. The larger crate held a steel-blue 1966 Bentley convertible. For the next six months, the couple could be seen on Sunday afternoons tooling sedately along the low road by the waterfront, he immaculate in seersucker and red paisley bow tie, she in the latest Mary Quant, fair hair tossing gently in the breeze set up by the automobile's smooth progress.

The small expatriate community of colonial officials and the striving local politicians of the Legislative Council welcomed Mr. and Mrs. Brooks with few questions and open arms. They were immediately included on the invitation list for all social events at the governor's residence and were equally at home at a local beach barbecue where they were the only white attendees. The statuesque Cybil and the debonair Nigel succeeded in charming all whom they encountered.

At all these social events, Nigel dropped subtle hints about his financial acumen and business connections, and before long the bureaucrats had dutifully spun them up to the point where he acquired a stature equivalent to that of the founders of the East India Company. When asked, Nigel suggested tourism as an antidote to the colony's anemic farming and fishing economy. He envisioned and described a future where the BVI would be the next Jamaica, the next Bahamas, and the crown jewel of Her Majesty's colonies in the Caribbean. The rising tide of tourism would lift all boats, with jobs, money, and entrepreneurial opportunity for every belonger.

The Legislative Council delegates had stars in their eyes. The colonial officials smelled a career boost, a ticket to a better posting, and maybe even a position at home in the Commonwealth Office, if the colony could be made to prosper on their watch. They all turned to Brooks for guidance and expertise.

Nigel played his marks coyly, temporizing until the tourism mania in the governing class reached a fever pitch. Finally, after months of entreaties from Government House, he and Cybil embarked on an all-islands tour of the colony for the purpose of evaluating its tourism and development potential.

At every stop, the couple was met with an enthusiasm that matched, if not exceeded, that shown for the visit of HRH Queen Elizabeth earlier in the year. Crowds of schoolchildren, waving small flags left over from the royal visit, awaited the Brookses as they disembarked at each island. Local dignitaries gave rambling recitations of their specific island's virtues as a potential destination for the tourist throngs sure to come. Nigel and Cybil modestly accepted it all as their due.

On completion of the tour, Nigel closeted himself in the suite at the Fort Burt Hotel for a month of deliberation and study of his notes. The Legislative Council and the Commonwealth Office functionaries waited in agitated anticipation. After the New Year holiday, Brooks addressed a packed session of the Legislative Council with his findings and recommendations.

The topography and population patterns of the BVI were a hindrance to large-scale development of tourism potential on most islands in the colony, Brooks declaimed. As volcanic islands, they had insufficient flat land to construct an airport large enough to accommodate the jet aircraft required for international flights from Europe and North America. Further, the clusters of small farming plots around suitable beaches and bays made land acquisition for resort development cost prohibitive and disruptive to the population.

Fortunately, one island did not suffer these impediments—Anegada. Its land was flat, and its interior could easily accommodate the eleven-thousand-foot runway needed to land the massive new Boeing 747 airliner. The population was small and concentrated in The Settlement, which would remain untouched by any resort development. The grand resort complexes would be built on the pristine beaches of the north shore, at Cow Wreck Bay, Bones Bight, Windlass Bight, and Jack Bay.

A hubbub began among the delegates to the Legislative Council and in the packed gallery. The thought of placing all the BVI's tourism eggs in the single remote basket of Anegada did not sit well with the representatives from Tortola, Virgin Gorda, and Jost Van Dyke, who had come to hear Nigel Brooks proclaim their respective home islands to be the centerpiece of a BVI tourism nascence.

Brooks had anticipated this reaction and was ready. A dignified request from him caused the speaker of the council to vigorously gavel the chamber to order. Brooks waited until the song of an ovenbird in the garden outside was the only sound to be heard. He then began a two-hour monologue, mixing hard facts with emotional appeals to patriotism, and paternalistic explanation with humor, hope, and tears. He ended by vowing to risk his entire fortune on the development of Anegada, as evidence of his faith in the plan he had formulated and the future of the people of the BVI. Despite the dry nature of the topic, the room erupted in shouts and cheers. Brooks, and Brooks's plan, had carried the day.

Lambs to the slaughter, the Legislative Council adopted the plan by acclamation. The Anegada Development Corporation was chartered by a special act of the council, with Nigel Brooks as its president and chief executive officer. The company was given a ninety-nine-year lease on all land west of The Settlement and along the entire north shore and east shore to the East End.

In the weeks that followed, the matter of financing was taken up in a series of legislative sessions. The Commonwealth Office bureaucrats, eager to assist, suggested an issue of development bonds backed by Her Majesty's Treasury. Benefited by a desultory regret the mother country was experiencing over its treatment of the colonies in the prior years, the proposal found sufficient support to land it on the desk of the chancellor of the Exchequer. At ten million pounds, the chancellor deemed the matter unworthy of more than cursory scrutiny. By mid-1967, HM Treasury consented to stand behind the bond issue.

Barclays bank provided the marketing horsepower, selling out the issue with lightning speed. Special provisions were made for the sale of small-denomination bonds in the BVI. In a rush of patriotism tinged with a hint of avarice, local sales approached one million pounds. Everyone in the colony invested. Those with savings too modest to purchase the lowest-denomination bonds on their own pooled their funds with neighbors and friends to buy a single bond together.

By Christmas 1967, the treasury of the BVI contained ten million pounds from the bond sales. Converted to US dollars, recently adopted as the currency for the BVI, this amounted to slightly more than $27 million.

The proximity of all that money in the same branch of Barclays bank that held the remains of his initial two-hundred-thousand-pound deposit must have set the black heart of Nigel Brooks a-pounding.

A lesser con man might have pushed for access to the

money, then and there, and probably could have made away with hundreds of thousands in quick order. Brooks, however, cemented his reputation as a prince among grifters by the patience he displayed when the prize of the Anegada con was so near. Brooks did not inquire about or attempt to get at the money. Instead, he set about doing exactly what he had promised to do.

First, Brooks spent his own funds to buy a used concrete batch plant in Puerto Rico. Two barges dropped the plant machinery and a Caterpillar D4 bulldozer at Setting Point on Commonwealth Day 1968. The bulldozer cut the first real road on Anegada, a gash through the scrub thorn from Setting Point to The Settlement. The road's purpose was to allow men from The Settlement to reach jobs at the batch plant.

Brooks hired every able-bodied man on Anegada who would work for him. None of the men had ever worked for hourly wages before. The concept of a regular starting and quitting time was alien to them. Most could not read or write. Despite these conditions, the batch plant was up and working in a month, using only one engineer from San Juan and local labor for the construction.

The bulldozer was then turned to the task of cutting a runway and airport grounds out of the bush in the center of the island. At the same time, concrete from the batch plant was used to build the ten-room Reef Hotel to house the first tourists and foreign investors. Once-sleepy Anegada fairly bustled with construction and promise.

Nigel and Cybil quit the Fort Burt Hotel, moving to

Anegada to supervise the construction. Their original accommodation was a sailboat on loan from the governor himself, anchored in the shallow bay at Setting Point. After the completion of the Reef Hotel, Brooks set his construction crew to work building a permanent home for him and Cybil. Known simply as the Villa, it was sited on a low rise just east of Pomato Point. A broad lawn of Bermuda grass, the first lawn on the island, flowed grandly from the shaded veranda of the Villa to the alabaster sand of the bay. Cybil passed the afternoons sunning on a chaise on the new grass, a chilled martini in hand.

Nigel spent his days in a flurry of activity. Morning might find him meeting with his construction foreman at the future Captain Auguste George Airport, followed by a midday boat trip to Road Town to make a progress report to the Legislative Council, and a session at the post office to send cables to materials suppliers and prospective operators for the resort. Every visit to Road Town ended in a meeting with the Barclays bank manager, with whom Nigel formed a warm and collegial relationship.

Working closely with his friend at Barclays, Nigel placed orders for millions of dollars of materials and furnishings for the planned resorts. Each cable confirmation of an order was immediately followed by a payment draft issued by the bank. The money was sprinkled to companies throughout the Caribbean, the US, and even South America. Twenty million dollars migrated from the Barclays bond account in a matter of months, with all disbursements approved over the willing signature of the branch manager.

The assembly of the many pieces needed to develop a world-class resort on remote Anegada occasionally required Nigel to venture outside the BVI. He would travel from Anegada to San Juan, and from there continue on to Mustique to meet with executives from Club Med or to Bogotá to confab with catering managers from Spain. He returned from these junkets with optimistic reports of impending proposals for partner relationships from those with whom he had met. The tourist boom, Nigel assured all who would listen, was just over the horizon.

As dollars flowed out of Barclays bank, precious little in the way of materials and furnishings found its way to Anegada. After the arrival of the batch plant and bulldozer, nothing came by barge at all. Some supplies were brought in from San Juan by air. But most of the items making the trip were not for the planned resort. Instead, only furniture for the Villa, tins of caviar, boxes of frozen steaks, and cases of Greenall's Special London Dry Gin, the latter being the principal ingredient in Cybil's favorite libation, made their way to Anegada.

After six months with no deliveries of building materials, polite inquiries were made by the chairman of the Legislative Council's Committee on Tourism and Development. Nigel provided prompt and plausible explanations for all the undelivered items. A strike in Pittsburgh had delayed the structural steel. An unfortunate fire at a furniture factory in North Carolina meant no beds or chairs for months. Kitchen equipment was back-ordered. There was a lumber shortage caused by labor problems in the southeastern United States.

The inquiries satisfied, Brooks returned to the business at hand. More orders were placed, and more drafts were issued by the Barclays branch manager. The good fellow had become so accommodating that on several occasions he bent the rules requiring paperwork in hand before sending payment, on the assertion from Nigel that a substantial discount would be lost if payment was not immediately made.

By the spring of 1970, Anegada had an unoccupied ten-room hotel, an airport with a gravel runway not yet approved for flight operations, and a new Italianate villa standing majestically on its south shore. The employees of the Anegada Development Corporation, though new to the world of wage-earning employment, began to question why their days were spent pushing piles of coral rock to and fro along the boundary of the airport property.

The development bond account at Barclays bank had been depleted to the tune of twenty-two million dollars. The loyal opposition in the Legislative Council demanded answers. The Committee on Tourism and Development scheduled a hearing, with a request that Nigel Brooks attend, for a day in late March.

The hearing time came and went, and Brooks did not appear. A check of the Villa and the Reef Hotel later that day failed to produce Nigel or Cybil. The beds in the Villa were neatly made, and champagne was still chilled in the refrigerator, but Mr. and Mrs. Brooks and their passports were gone.

Rumors of a night flight from the untested runway at the airport circulated.

A stormy session of the Legislative Council followed. Accusations and counter-accusations of laxity, neglect, and corruption were made and rebutted. In the end, the council ordered an accounting and referred the matter to the fledgling Royal Virgin Islands Police Force. Five million dollars remained on deposit at Barclays, and several hundred thousand dollars were known to have been expended for materials actually received. The balance of the bond issue proceeds, slightly more than twenty-one million dollars, had vanished along with Nigel and Cybil.

After six months, Cybil was traced to Fez, Morocco, where she had opened a gentlemen's club featuring a stable of blond entertainers, male and female, from Sweden, Norway, and Denmark. Possible extradition was considered and then abandoned by the Office of the Director of Public Prosecutions. There was no evidence that Cybil had committed any crime while in the BVI.

Nigel Brooks was charged with almost every fraud crime available under English common law. He proved more elusive than Cybil but ultimately surfaced in Brazil after two years. With no extradition treaty between Brazil and the United Kingdom, the colony's law enforcement community stood helplessly by while Nigel engaged in a decade-long public party on the beaches and in the nightclubs of Rio de Janeiro. In 1980, his seventeen-year-old mistress stabbed him to death in a fit of pique after Nigel announced that he was leaving her for a younger woman.

While Nigel Brooks had been a hard partier, living in Brazil, even living very well, was cheap in the seventies. Brooks's lifestyle was such that it was clear he had squandered no more than a few million dollars during his decade in Rio. The unspent millions had never been found.

Chapter Twenty-Five

I took a breath and plunged in. The waters would be deep and dangerous, but it had to be done. "Dada, how do you know Nigel Brooks used helicopters?"

"I saw them. Saw them with my own eyes. And heard about them from some of the boys in town who worked for Brooks. They used the steel matting at the old tracking station as a landing platform. Once a week a helicopter would come in with supplies for Brooks and that woman of his. All the supplies were luxury items. I remember Rot Faulkner telling me about unloading five whole cases of gin for that woman's martini habit."

Rot Faulkner. My own father-in-law, dead these two years past. I thought to myself that some helpful information probably died with him.

Dada continued. "I didn't see any of the gin myself, since I never worked for Brooks."

"Did you ever meet the helicopter pilots?"

"No. I only saw them at a distance. A black man and a white man."

"Do you remember the name of the helicopter charter company?"

"I don't think I ever knew it." Dada squinted, seemed to look back in time. "The helicopter was green, a military green, kind of drab. It was old and beat-up; maybe it was bought as surplus. There was no company name written on it but it did have this weird emblem painted on the door, really odd, a hamburger with wings on it. Like a flying hamburger. It's funny how something like that will stick in your mind, even after all these years."

Just like "Hamburger 5," the call sign of John Ippolito and Neville Wells's helicopter, was now stuck in my mind. The flying-hamburger emblem on the helicopter shuttling caviar and gin to Nigel Brooks on Anegada couldn't be a coincidence. Like the poor policeman I am, I felt the connection in my bones with no real evidence, intuition without a shred of substantiation.

Dada let his attention drift, his thoughts probably lost somewhere in 1970s Anegada. His eyes had a faraway look. I could see we were done.

"Give Madda my best, Dada," I said.

"I will, Teddy." His eyes snapped back into focus. "And then I'll give her my best!" A lecherous leer spread slowly across his face.

Too much information, Dada.

The tropical sunset had ended, snapping the day shut like a drawn shade, by the time I reached the administration building. I fired up Pamela Pickering's desktop computer for the second time of the day.

Three minutes on Google, and I was roaming the records of the secretary of state for the Commonwealth of Puerto Rico. Three minutes more and I had located the information for Hamburger 5 Air Charters Inc. The corporation had had its charter revoked in 1972 for nonpayment of the annual registration fee. A click to another page gave the date and place of incorporation, December 19, 1968, in San Juan, and the name of the principal incorporator, Neville Wells. The company had even registered a trademark, described in the mark application as "a graphic depiction of a hamburger meat patty in a bun, with two feathered wings projecting from the sides of the bun." Another twenty minutes on the website garnered no further information.

What I knew now was significant and not mere gut speculation. I knew the dead Professor Paul Kelliher was really John Ippolito and was not a professor. I knew John Ippolito had served in Vietnam with Neville Wells. I knew that Neville Wells had operated a helicopter charter service in San Juan in the late 1960s and, if my father's memory was to be trusted, had worked for the infamous Nigel Brooks. I knew that Brooks had absconded with millions of dollars that were never recovered. I knew that Ippolito/Kelliher had spent years on Anegada searching for something. I knew that Neville Wells's daughter, Cat, had appeared on Anegada short months ago.

I knew that Cat Wells was my lover, mistress, paramour, inamorata; pick a term.

I did not know how all of it fit together. And I did not know how I was going to find out.

Warm light shone from the big kitchen windows of my house as I pulled the RVIPF Land Rover to the stony parking spot at its rear. The comforting clatter of plates, pots, and happy voices greeted me through the open screen door. I was tired on top of a layer of tired, and a midnight shift at the power plant awaited me. I hoped a good meal and the pleasant diversion of family time, domestic and mundane, would restore me enough to get through the coming night.

Icilda had a smile and a chaste offering of her cheek to peck as a greeting. No excessive displays of affection were permitted in front of the kids, which, given my current state of romantic involvement with someone other than Icilda, suited me just fine.

Icilda's cheek smelled of curry, her seasoning for the pumpkin soup that would accompany baked wahoo and coconut rice and peas as the evening meal. She had learned to make coconut rice and peas from my mother when we were first married. The memory sent a mixed twinge of pleasure and guilt through me, pleasure that she still took the trouble to make my favorite dish, and guilt that I was being unfaithful to her while she still cared for me in some way.

"Sit down, Teddy. You must be tired. The food will be on in just a minute," Icilda said, her voice soft with concern. She was in full mothering mode. "I'm worried you're working too hard lately."

"It's just all this stuff piling up, the murder, De Rasta's beating, and it needs to be solved. *I* need to solve it and I have to work hard to solve it. My reputation and my job are on the line." Each word I said felt like added weight placed on my shoulders. I sagged in my chair.

Icilda set a steaming bowl of pumpkin soup before me. "You want iced tea?"

"Yes, thanks. The thing is, I know it won't come out right, the truth won't come out, unless I solve it." What a hypocrite you are, Teddy Creque, talking to the wife you are cheating on about the truth. "I think I'm close to something but I don't know what."

Icilda poured a tall glass of tea. "What do you mean, Teddy? What are you close to?" she asked with mild interest. Tamia and Kevin were silent and attentive. The events of the last few days were the only topic of conversation on Anegada, even at school. They had a ringside seat and were eager for information.

"I think there is a connection between the murder and Nigel Brooks," I said. And between the murder and the woman I am sleeping with behind your back. The pumpkin soup, creamy and pungent, suddenly tasted bitter on my tongue.

Kevin and Tamia leaned in. As young as they were, they knew the Brooks name and the story of the missing millions. You could not grow up on Anegada without knowing.

"What kind of connection?" Icilda said, her expression betraying mild disbelief.

"I don't know. But there is a connection and I have to work hard to put it together. I talked to Dada this afternoon, trying to get information about when Brooks was here. He was helpful but he only knew so much because he was one of the few men on Anegada at the time who didn't work for Brooks. He even mentioned your father, Icilda, and some of the things he said about working for Brooks. Did Rot ever talk to you about Brooks before he passed?"

"Poppa was a crew foreman on the airport and the road construction crew, and he talked about building those things, but he never said much about Brooks. Except that he was a crook who stole the future of Anegada and all the people here," Icilda said.

"Did Rot ever talk about how supplies were brought in for Brooks's project?"

"No. Well, yes, he said the concrete plant and the equipment to build the road were brought in by barge from San Juan but that's all I remember. Mostly he talked about what fools they all were, to be taken in by Brooks and his promises of turning Anegada into a tourist resort. A godless man, for sure." Icilda spat out the last words, as if trying to expel a bad taste from her mouth.

"Did he mention anything about supplies being flown in?"

"No. How could that be, with the airport not open?"

"By helicopter. Did he say anything about people or supplies coming in by helicopter?"

"No." Icilda's expression was blank. "Are you done with your soup? I made your favorite, coconut rice and peas."

Icilda rose to the stove and began to fill plates. Kevin and

Tamia, sensing the possibility of learning any more information had been exhausted, launched into a sibling argument over after-dinner television rights. The dinner conversation turned to school, Icilda's work, and, of course, church matters. I was able to nap for an hour before my shift at the power plant.

Chapter Twenty-Six

Many a day on Anegada begins in less than perfect circumstances. The sunburn from snorkeling or the hangover from last night's rum smoothies at the Reef Hotel bar has often made for a hard start to a tourist's day. A double shift waiting tables, a night hauling fish traps, or an evening with the selfsame rum smoothies has done the same for those of us who are belongers. But the soft Anegada morning usually heals the ills of the previous day, or night. The agreeable breeze, scented with sea and frangipani, clears the head. The forenoon sun is mild and soothing. The palms provide perspective.

So it was for me on this day. The cranky machinery at the power plant had deprived me of hoped-for rest. I dragged out the plant door at first light, only to be renewed by the matchless Anegada daybreak on the brief walk to the administration building. There was a spring in my step by the time I reached the front entrance. To my surprise, Pamela Pickering was already in. She completed my revivification by presenting me with a steaming mug of coffee.

The coffee was fresh and bracingly black. Pamela could make a great cup, if she put her mind to it. She made a pot for herself most days, shortly after she rolled in at midmorning. Today she was in at dawn and had made a pot just for me. Something was wrong.

Pamela watched me take the first sip like a prison guard watching a condemned man dig into his last meal.

"Teddy, I got to talk to you about a call I got yesterday." Pamela hesitated, rare for her and a true indication of her discomfort. Normally, a Niagara of speech flowed from her lips, little or none of it detouring through her brain along the way.

"Go ahead."

"I got a call from Tortola, Teddy. From Helen Smith-Williams. She the assistant secretary to the deputy governor and it was a call on official business. She ask me for a recommendation, Teddy, for who I would recommend from Anegada to be trained as a special constable. She ask me not to tell anybody but I thought you should know."

"What did you tell her when she asked for a recommendation?" I said.

Pamela squared her shoulders and looked me in the eye. "I told her she don' need a recommendation, the special constable we have now do a fine job."

"Thank you, Pamela."

"I meant it." The torrent unleashed. "They can't do that to you, Teddy. What happening here, the dead man and De Rasta beating, ain't not your fault. I don' know what we do without you. They just get some fool from The Settlement, like—"

I held up my hand, not wanting to hear. The utterance of my replacement's name would only make my departure seem closer. And it seemed very close already.

"Not to worry, Pamela. I'll get this worked out yet, and there won't be a new special constable. Thanks for the coffee and the heads-up." I tried to sound reassuring. Pamela nodded and sniffed back the start of tears, returning to her office. She seemed a good deal more reassured than I was.

The handwriting, if it had not been before, was certainly on the wall now. My days on the Royal Virgin Islands Police Force were numbered. Come to think of it, it was amazing I was not gone already. And in my bones I felt close to another thing, close to linking Neville Wells to Nigel Brooks to John Ippolito. To Cat Wells. I could sit back and wait for the fateful call from Deputy Commissioner Lane or I could keep digging, scrabbling, trying to work out the whys and the wherefores. I chose the latter course, mainly because action was preferable to inaction. One of life's most attractive fictions is the folly of control over one's own fate.

Coffee in hand, I eased into the hard chair behind my desk and found myself for—what?—the third, fourth, tenth time in this case with nowhere to turn next and no plan of action. Think, Teddy; how do real police officers go about solving crimes? I've seen enough cop shows since satellite TV came to Anegada to do this. Evidence, witnesses, motive, opportunity, suspects. The words whirled around in my head. It was easy for Detective Briscoe on *Law & Order* and Detective Chief Superintendent Foyle on *Foyle's War*. They dug and probed, questioned and considered, and by dint of good police work and an uncanny ability to read people, they established motive and opportunity, and located evidence and witnesses, until the crime was solved and justice done. Simple. I just needed to list what I had and work from there.

Physical evidence first. I had no murder weapon. No bullet or casing from the murder weapon. No weapon used in the assault on Anthony Wedderburn. I had a handwritten map to who knows what. A coded notebook, undeciphered, now missing.

Motive next. Drugs, if you believed DC Lane's theory. Treasure, if you believed Wendell George's actions. Something left on Anegada by Nigel Brooks, if you believed my gut. No support for any of them.

Opportunity. On the murder, everyone on Anegada at the time. On the assault, the same. Also, on both, maybe a person or persons who had come and gone without the knowledge of anyone other than the victim.

Witnesses. Belle Lloyd, but I had spoken to her twice and she was peripheral at best. Paul Kelliher/John Ippolito, now dead. Neville Wells, now dead. Nigel Brooks, now dead. Anthony Wedderburn, in a coma at Peebles Hospital.

Suspects. Cat Wells, though I could not articulate why.

Maybe I was due for some luck. Maybe the one witness who was still alive would be out of his coma. Maybe Lord Anthony Wedderburn, De White Rasta, the ganja-addled code breaker, would be waiting in his comfortable hospital bed for my call.

I dialed Peebles Hospital and was quickly put through to the two-bed Intensive Care Unit.

"Intensive Care, Nurse Rowell." The voice at the end of the line was no-nonsense, with a clipped Abaco accent. It was the voice of a nurse who could put a young doctor in his place if she felt it necessary.

"Nurse Rowell, this is Special Constable Teddy Creque of the Royal Virgin Islands Police Force on Anegada. I'm calling to inquire about the condition of a crime victim who is a patient in the ICU, Anthony Wedderburn," I said, straight to the point and all business. I hoped Nurse Rowell would appreciate that approach.

"Constable, I was just about to call your Inspector Stoutt to report what had occurred with that patient during the night."

"I am working with Inspector Stoutt on the case," I said. It was mostly true. Well, it contained a grain of truth. "What is Mr. Wedderburn's status?"

"Mr. Wedderburn remains in grave condition but he did show some signs yesterday that he might be able to breathe on his own without remaining intubated. We began reducing his dosage of propofol yesterday morning, hoping to bring him to the point where he could be taken off the ventilator.

Shortly after midnight he regained consciousness. Unfortunately, he became agitated due to the presence of the breathing tube and he had to be placed back under sedation."

"Was he able to speak while he was conscious?"

"The breathing tube prevented him from speaking," Nurse Rowell explained, allowing a practiced trace of exasperation into her voice at my medical ignorance. "He did, however, gesture for a pen and paper and managed to write one word before he became agitated. He wrote 'shag,' Constable, S-H-A-G. Quite remarkable, isn't it, that a man undergoes an extreme trauma, is barely clinging to life, and his first thought when he regains consciousness is to ask for a smoke. But, then again, tobacco is the most addictive of all habit-forming substances."

"That was all he wrote, 'shag'?"

"Yes, Constable. It was quite clear. We have saved the paper, if you would like to see it."

"Thank you, that won't be necessary. So Mr. Wedderburn remains in a coma?"

"Yes. He is still intubated and breathing on the ventilator. Would you like to be contacted if his condition changes? Inspector Stoutt has already asked that we contact him but I see no reason why we cannot contact you both. You two seem to be the only ones interested in the gentleman's condition."

"Thank you, no, that won't be necessary. I may call in periodically for an update."

"Will you inform Inspector Stoutt about Mr. Wedderburn's status or do I need to call him?"

"I will let him know, Nurse Rowell. Thank you."

"You're welcome, Constable." The connection went dead.

I thought about not calling Rollie. There was really nothing to report other than De Rasta's yearning for homegrown tobacco and the pessimistic news of his return to the twilight of induced coma. But information was information and I had learned the lesson of not reporting it when a report was expected. Besides, Rollie might have something for me.

The audible sigh before Rollie spoke told me he was approaching the day with his usual enthusiasm. After a perfunctory greeting in both directions, I relayed what I had learned from Nurse Rowell.

"Shag? What does that mean? Carpet or homegrown?" Rollie sounded almost, but not quite, interested.

"Homegrown. He grows his own and smokes it when he's not burning something more potent."

"The man is nearly killed, finally comes out of a coma, and all he can think about is lighting up a fatty? Incredible."

"He may have been a little fuzzy from his injuries."

"You think so? Maybe he's permanently fuzzy from all the ganja the DC says he smokes." Inspector Stoutt had obviously been discussing the case with DC Lane. I wondered if he had bought the RVIPF party line that Anegada's crime problem was drug related.

"Do you think a visit to Peebles would be worthwhile?" I asked, hoping to gently nudge Rollie into making the epic journey of a quarter mile from police headquarters to the hospital.

"Not if the guy's in a coma and writing crazy stuff when

he comes out of it," Rollie said with his usual reluctance to become involved in anything resembling the actual investigation of a case to which he had been assigned. Some things do not change.

"Any other news?" I asked, hoping something, anything, other than disappointment with Inspector Stoutt, would come out of our conversation.

"Agent Rosenblum and his JITFS boys are still in town, shaking the trees to find out who the drug lord of Anegada is. Other than that, no new news. Jeezum, the DC's on the other line. I gotta go."

I dropped the phone receiver into its cradle. A dove cooed outside the window. The morning had turned hot and still. Pamela Pickering was weeping softly in her office down the hall. I closed my eyes to consider my options and narrowed them to two. I could go to Cat and hope to shake things loose through subterfuge or confrontation, or I could wait in my office, listening to the weeping and cooing, and hope for a break to drop in my lap.

The choice was easy. Waiting for a break in this case might take the rest of my life, or, at the very least, the rest of my career with the RVIPF. And I wasn't that fond of doves or crying women.

Chapter Twenty-Seven

The teak-panel front door of Frangipani House opened slightly in response to my knock, revealing a single emerald-green eye. For an instant, the eye betrayed concern on the part of its owner, but only for an instant. By the time the door was fully open, the eye and its owner were coolly composed.

"Come in, lover," Cat literally purred. The words were right, the tone was right. It felt all wrong.

I stepped into the tiled foyer. An overnight bag was packed and waiting at the foot of the stairs. The lovely emerald eye and its companion tracked my glance toward the bag.

"I am so glad you came, Teddy. I was just going to try to reach you. One of the other pilots at VI Birds broke his leg, fell off a bar stool in St. Thomas, can you believe it, and they need me to take his charters for the rest of the week. Looks like my little vacation has been cut short. They're sending a plane over in half an hour. I'm so disappointed, lover. I was hoping we could have some more time together before I had to go."

She leaned into me, pushed up on her toes, turned her face up. The lovely emerald eyes closed, slowly and with well-rehearsed sensuality. Her lips tested mine and parted, allowing her tongue to dart and explore. "I'll make it up to you, Teddy. Let's start now. We have a few minutes before I have to leave for the airport." Her hand strayed below my waist, caressing.

The ache of desire rose in me. I heard myself groan from the back of my throat. Cat worked industriously down the front of my body, kissing my neck, then my chest, pulling out the tails of my uniform shirt from the front of my shorts.

What the hell am I doing? I'm not sure if I actually said it or just heard it inside my head. Cat was on her knees, diligently prying at my belt buckle, when I stepped back. One step, but it might as well have been a mile. For me, Cat's spell was broken.

For Cat, it did not quite register. In a sultry murmur, she said, "Don't worry. We have time. They can wait on the runway for a few minutes." She reached out for the buckle. I took another step back.

"I need to talk to you about John Ippolito."

The lovely eyes played Judas to their master for half a heartbeat. "Who is John Ippolito?" Cat asked, all puzzled innocence.

"He flew with your father in Vietnam. He was your father's business partner in his air charter business in San Juan after the war."

"Teddy, what are you talking about? I don't know anything about that. I wasn't even born. And I've never heard of John Ippolito."

"He was killed at Spanish Camp last week. He was traveling under an assumed identity as Professor Paul Kelliher. Why would he be doing that?"

"How should I know that, Teddy?"

"You visited him while he was out at Spanish Camp, didn't you? You flew supplies to him at sunset a few times a month. You know, the unscheduled landings you made that weren't cleared through customs."

"I don't know what you're talking about." Cat shook her head in mock disbelief. "This is crazy, lover. This is just crazy."

"Didn't you fly to Spanish Camp? I'm sure we could check with the US Customs and Border Patrol about the flight plans you filed for the last few months."

"Are you calling me a liar? Just because I may have taken a few sightseeing tours around the island without landing?"

I said nothing.

Cat rose from her knees, pulling herself to her full height at the same time she worked herself into a state of anger. A state of feigned anger, contrived and calculated.

"I don't have to take this from you! You have no reason to call me a liar. Just because you have no lead in your case is no reason to start picking on me." The lovely eyes flashed sham anger while studying me closely to measure the effect.

It had none. We stood apart for a long cold moment.

Cat decided to escalate. "You ungrateful bastard! I come

to this godforsaken rock and show you a little fun and this is the thanks I get? You're lucky I gave you the time of day, you rube, with your tattered clothes and your cheesy story about your wife not understanding you. You're the liar, but I went along with it because I wanted the sex. That's right, I wanted the sex, just for my amusement, and you were convenient. Convenient and not even that good. Not that it wasn't the biggest thrill of your pathetic bumpkin life. Well, I'm done with you, Teddy. Done with sneaking around this sand pile to service you. Done with hiding from your holier-than-thou wife. I wasn't getting much out of it in the first place and now all I seem to be getting is accused. You can take your accusation and shove it. I've got a flight to catch."

Cat moved toward the bag by the stairs. As she did, I reached out and caught her by the elbow, bringing her up short. She turned and slapped me with her free hand, hard.

I had been slapped before. Madda cuffed me once or twice because I brought home and used a word I had heard whispered on the playground at school. Another time, on the same playground, I stole a preadolescent kiss from Judy Soares and received a swat that was more "come hither" than "back off." But the blow Cat delivered was a new experience for me, an ear-ringing wallop inflicted for decisive effect.

It worked. Cat twisted her elbow free and was quickly out the door with her bag. I stepped out in time to see the approach of the VI Birds Piper Aztec from the south. It must have cleared customs in Tortola, at Lettsome International Airport, so I was not informed it would be arriving. Cat flung her bag into the passenger seat of her car and lit out for the airport, the rear tires of the Mitsubishi scattering bits of crushed coral against the fender of my Land Rover.

I did not follow. There was no reason to follow. I understood she would not speak to me except to evade. Her actions confirmed her involvement—some involvement—in whatever had brought Ippolito/Kelliher to Anegada but I could not hold her on suspicion of her involvement in something to which I could put no name or explanation.

Having carried out and mucked up my brilliant investigative strategy for the morning, I decided it was best to move in the opposite direction from the airport. Perhaps an hour at Walkover Set Bay, boring holes in the waves with my eyeballs, would clear my head and provide direction for my next effort. But before I made the turn off the lonely north shore road toward the bay, my destination changed. The washboard pounding of the road must have jarred some sense into me because I finally realized De White Rasta's scrawled note to Nurse Rowell was not a request to her for a cigarette.

It was a message to me.

Chapter Twenty-Eight

Just before the little bridge over the mouth of Bumber Well Pond, there is a turnoff with barely enough room to park a single vehicle among the mangroves. The turnoff was unoccupied that morning. The turnoff was always unoccupied. Nobody ever went to Saltheap Point.

I realized I would make my first visit to Saltheap Point in years when I grasped that Anthony Wedderburn's communication of the word "shag" was not a request but a reference to a place. The place was Saltheap Point, the location of De Rasta's shag patch.

Navigating the short path from the turnoff, I was reminded of the reasons why nobody went to Saltheap. The scrub thorn was dense, pricking and plucking at my clothing and skin. Hand-sized spiders decorated the bushes with gossamer webs. Mosquitoes circled and droned. The ground, if it could be called that, was a slippery amalgam of decaying plant matter and brackish effluent from the nearby salt pond. The hot air was putrid with sulfur, rotten seaweed, and dead mullet. Not exactly Disney World.

The path ended at a flat mud beach. The mosquitoes hung back in the foliage, biding their time until my return trip. Turning west, I saw De Rasta's shag patch a stone's throw away.

It wasn't much. Three rows of yellowing tobacco plants, elevated on earthen mounds, stood listlessly under the unblinking sun. A few racks made of mangrove sticks dried the most recent harvest in the shade of a palm-frond lean-to. A circular limestone sinkhole appeared to be the water supply. A five-gallon paint bucket with a dipper made from a plastic bleach bottle stood beside the sink.

I picked up the bucket, examined it, put it down again. A tour around the drying racks and lean-to revealed nothing. No information could be divined from the sinkhole, after some minutes of peering into the turgid water. It might have helped if I had known what I was searching for but I did not. I only knew that De Rasta felt it was important that I find it and that it would be found in this place.

The shag patch itself was next. I walked it row by row, a solitary general reviewing the ranks of wilting tobacco troops. De Rasta had marked each corner boundary of the patch with a weathered piece of coral. On the edge of the patch closest to the sea, the marker was a slab of brain coral. I almost missed it, so faint were the lines, but the letters "TC," newly etched in the coral, caught my eye.

I picked up the coral and looked at the underside. Nothing. The soggy ground beneath it seemed undisturbed but I took a driftwood stick and poked at it anyway. The stick struck something solid with a hollow thunk. Digging with my bare hands in the mud produced a jar with a metal lid. The scrap of label clinging to it read MATOUK'S PICKLED PEPPERS.

I carried the jar to the water and washed the mud from it. Inside was a sheaf of notebook papers, covered in Anthony Wedderburn's practiced public school cursive. I drew the papers out, unfolded them, and read the top page:

Hello, Teddy,

Last night, as I worked late, I heard noises outside the church which have me jumpy and a touch paranoid. It is probably nothing. While my presence at the church is no secret, I have told no one of the nature of my work for you and I assume you have not either. Nonetheless, I think it prudent to make an extra copy of what I have done to date and leave it here for you in the event my paranoia is not unfounded.

If you are reading this, old man, the news cannot be good for me. Please know that whatever may have befallen me is not your fault. Any risk involved in my working for you was undertaken with open eyes.

Know too that the work on this project has made me feel more vital and my life more meaningful than anything I have done in the past twenty years. For this you have my genuine gratitude.

Hope you solve it, old chap!

Your Friend,

Anthony

Below this first sheet were half a dozen others, also in De Rasta's hand. While they were not labeled as the text of the coded notebook, their content left little doubt:

My Dearest Mary Catherine,

The doctors now tell me they have diagnosed my problem. I will not bore you with the details. They say I will die any day now unless I have open-heart surgery, and even then I will be restricted in my activities and probably be an invalid for the rest of my life.

I will not let those cold-blooded butchers cut me open. I will take my chances with the ticker that the Good Lord gave me. It has served me adequately until now and I would rather die than spend my last years in a rocking chair or a nursing home bed anyway.

If what the quack bastards say is correct, I may not be here when you return from your service to our country. I do not have much to leave you in the way of material goods. Business and money have never been my strengths. The only real success in my life has been to raise a beautiful, intelligent, and talented daughter. I like to think that a small part of your many good qualities comes from what I have taught you or shown by way of example. You are the pride and joy of this old soldier, and I love you.

While there is no material wealth to leave you, I can leave you a chance at wealth, or what I believe to be wealth, hidden on a Caribbean island called Anegada. I know this sounds like the old pirate's-treasure games we used to play when you were a kid, but it is no game. The pirate involved never sailed the sea to plunder and rob; he was a modern-day buccaneer, a con man, named Nigel Brooks. The treasure is a product of the con he pulled off and should be in the millions.

I had hoped to find the treasure myself but life, and, it appears now, death, intervened. You must have found my note to you and the key to the code allowing you to read these words. I am sorry to be so mysterious but I wanted to make certain that you, and only you, would be able to use this information.

Here is what happened and what I can tell you about the treasure.

You know you were born on Puerto Rico. Your mother and I were there because, after I got out of the army in '66, Johnny Ipp and I decided to start an air charter business. Johnny thought the Caribbean was going to explode with tourism and a helicopter charter service would do well there. He scouted the islands and persuaded me that San Juan was the place to be. We set up a company named after our old call sign from Nam, Hamburger 5 Air Charters. We scrounged up a surplus Huey and we were in business.

The problem was, we didn't know how to get cus-

tomers. In a matter of months, we were about to lose everything.

Then one day a fellow named Nigel Brooks showed up at our cubbyhole office at the hangar, dressed to the nines like someone's idea of a yachtsman. He said he didn't have time to take a boat back to his place in the British Virgin Islands and asked if we could fly him there. We jumped at the chance. It didn't hurt that he paid in cash.

We had never heard of Anegada before that day and had never flown to the BVI. There was no airport on Anegada, no real roads, and there was a shack town that looked no better than an in-country hamlet in Nam. We landed on a beach on the south side of the island, near a big house Brooks was building for himself and his wife.

Brooks spent most of the trip from San Juan jabbering about the plans he had for Anegada. He said he was in the process of developing the island as a luxury resort. At the end of the flight, he asked if we would be able to procure and transport supplies from SJ to Anegada once a week, and occasionally fly him from Anegada to SJ for meetings. He offered cash in advance, then and throughout the time we worked for him.

That began more than a year of flights by Johnny Ipp and me to Brooks's house or to an abandoned American radar tracking station on the island. We had a regular weekly supply flight and a steady income from Brooks and his project. It was enough to keep us in business and keep food on the table.

Then one day Brooks approached me just after we landed on a supply run and asked if I would accompany him and one of the locals on a boat trip that evening and then fly Mrs. Brooks to SJ. It was the first time he had asked us to do anything other than flying but he was our good and only steady customer, so I agreed. Johnny and I hung around that afternoon, killing time swimming and sleeping in the shade of the Huey.

At dusk, Brooks appeared in khaki pants and shirt, carrying a bag made of shagreen, a kind of leather tanned from sharkskin. It looked like an old-style dispatch bag. I walked to the end of the short dock in front of the house with Brooks while Johnny Ipp stayed with the aircraft.

In a few minutes, one of the local men, whose name I did not know, approached from the east in a small fishing boat fitted with an ancient three-horsepower outboard motor. I helped Brooks down off the dock into the boat and climbed in after him. Brooks sat in the stern seat next to the local. I sat in the bow seat to balance the boat. Brooks spoke to the local but his words were lost in the sound of the outboard.

Brooks seemed nervous about the bag, clutching it tightly even when seated in the boat. He had not said it but it was my impression that he did not entirely trust the local. Perhaps he believed if I was along the local would not try anything.

We left the dock, turning south for a few hundred yards, and then ran straight east. The sunset had been dramatic, with large cumulus clouds on the horizon. As night closed in, more clouds appeared, blocking out the stars. The moon had not risen yet and consequently it was soon pitch-dark. There were no lights on the little boat. I could not see the south shore of the island, but it seemed like we were running parallel to it. The old outboard was unmuffled and it drowned out all other sounds. We continued for a good hour, then swung north for a few minutes, and with a final loop a few yards west, we pulled into the shallows along a white sand beach.

The local cut the engine, jumped over the stern into knee-deep water, and pushed the boat further toward the beach until it grounded. Brooks stepped into water barely covering his ankles and waded onto the beach, still clenching his bag. I followed with the local, dragging the boat onto the shore. By now a full moon was rising at the sky's edge. The heavy clouds parted and then rejoined, allowing a fleeting glimpse of the shore, empty but for flotsam and jetsam, and the dune ridge beyond.

Brooks said, "Be back shortly," as if he was going out for a stroll; marched across the beach, up and over the dune; and disappeared. The local yanked a corked pint of rum from his pocket and perched against the gunwale of the boat. He seemed to think we would be there for a while. He offered me a pull on the bottle but no conversation.

I sat on the sand. Long minutes passed. The moon moved in and out of the clouds, taking us from pitch black to daylight bright as it rose in the sky.

I asked the local the name of the place we were at. He said, "The Camp of the Great Admiral," as if that explained all, and fell silent again. I did not pursue it further. The man obviously did not want to talk, and anyway, the beach was as unremarkable and unidentifiable as the miles of similar beach girdling the island.

We waited for an hour before the figure of Brooks reappeared, cresting the dune and picking his way along the beach. The moon broke from a veil of cloud as he reached us. He no longer carried the bag. Coming up to the side of the boat, he brushed against me. He was wet from head to foot, even though he had only gone in to the top of his ankles coming ashore. I thought he might have fallen into a salt pond on the inland side of the dune but then I rubbed my finger against my arm where he had come in contact with me and tasted. It was freshwater.

Brooks and the local immediately dragged the bow of the boat seaward, while I pushed. When the boat floated, we jumped in and the local started the motor. The moon was completely visible now and I could see that the local had targeted a gap in the waves breaking over the reef. After piloting us expertly through, he angled northward into the Anegada Trench. In a quarter of an hour, an unlighted shape appeared on the horizon. In another quarter hour, the shape had sharpened into a bedraggled two-masted schooner.

The local killed the engine two hundred yards from the sailboat. A searchlight beam was shined directly at us. Brooks called out in Spanish, saying he was "Mr. Smithson" and he was ready to come aboard. The light blinked out, the outboard was restarted, and we pulled alongside.

Brooks turned to me and asked again for Johnny and me to take his wife to SJ on our return trip. He pushed a soggy wad of fifty-dollar bills into my hand, saying that it should cover the evening's work and his wife's airfare. A rope ladder was tossed over the rail of the sailboat and Brooks climbed aboard. I never saw him again.

The local remained mute on the return. He deposited me at the short dock without even tying up and turned to the west as soon as I had clambered out. By then it was nearing midnight but Mrs. Brooks popped out the door as I approached the house, traveling bag in hand. By two in the morning, we had cleared customs in SJ. Mrs. Brooks roused a dozing taxi driver at the terminal entrance and sped off into the night.

Two days later, I learned that Mr. and Mrs. Brooks were wanted by the BVI police for questioning about the disappearance of millions of dollars earmarked by the government for the development of Anegada. A week later, I heard the BVI authorities were seeking the helicopter crew who had aided the Brookses in their escape. Neither Johnny Ipp nor I was anxious to put ourselves in the hands of the island cops. We had seen enough of what the third-world fuzz would do watching the canh sat *at work in Vietnam. We assumed that we, like Brooks and his wife, were officially or unofficially regarded as fugitives in the BVI and we never returned there.*

That is what I know, little one. What I speculate is that the bag Nigel Brooks carried over the dune at "the Camp of the Great Admiral" contained something of immense value. I heard Brooks showed up later in Brazil, lived high on the hog for a few years, and died there. The BVI cops never got him and most of the money he took was never found. They say that he took enough to last a man ten lifetimes in South America and that he could not have spent it all. I think the bag contained the rest of the money, or the means to get it. I think whatever was in that bag is still on Anegada. Go and find it.

Keep in mind that Johnny Ipp knows some of what I tell you here, but not all of it. I never told him the whole story of that evening and

And there the manuscript ended. Just as well, as my attention was diverted by the thrum of helicopter blades. Fifty feet off the water's surface to the south, a mango-yellow VI Birds chopper headed straight for Captain Auguste George Airport, traveling fast.

Chapter Twenty-Nine

Even as I slipped and slid down the narrow mud beach, I knew there was no way I could reach the airport in time to intercept Cat. Still, I ran the path from beach to road as fast as I could, thorns tearing at my arms and legs, rivulets of sweat drenching me in the scorching afternoon sun. I pushed the Land Rover to fifty miles per hour on the washboard sand-and-coral road, at the edge of control on the broken surface. A gaunt cow and calf wandered into the intersection of the unpaved road with the concrete airport drive; I slewed off the shoulder and missed them by inches.

When I ground to a halt in the dusty terminal parking lot, Cat's rented Mitsubishi was not there, nor were any other vehicles. Walking around the empty terminal revealed the VI Birds Bell 429 in the far corner of the aircraft taxi area. The ticking and clicking of the cooling engine greeted me as

I approached. I placed my hands on the sides of my face to screen reflection and peered into the cockpit. I recognized Cat's overnight bag there, stowed behind the pilot's seat.

There were decisions to make and I made them. There were actions to take and I took them.

The last decision, and the corollary action, sent me on the road north toward Loblolly High Point and Flash of Beauty. I assumed Cat had preceded me by minutes. After reading De White Rasta's manuscript, I knew there was no reason for Cat to go elsewhere. It all fell into place. Cat and Ippolito/Kelliher were working together to find the mysterious treasure that Nigel Brooks had hidden at Spanish Camp. There must have been a dispute between them and Cat had killed Ippolito. But the treasure had not been found. Cat had taken the risk of returning to Anegada for the contents of the shagreen bag Brooks had deposited at the Camp of the Great Admiral. I knew I would find her at Spanish Camp. I would arrest her there for Ippolito's murder and the assault on Anthony Wedderburn.

The paved part of the airport road ended a quarter mile north of the airport driveway. After leaving the pavement, I weaved and juked, trying to find the least horrible route between potholes. At the same time, I grabbed the CB microphone and called Pamela Pickering.

"Yes, Teddy." Pamela's voice was raspy and wounded from her earlier crying jag.

"Switch to the alternate channel, Pamela," I said. No need to make this more public than necessary.

Clicking over to channel 20, Pamela greeted me with "I'm here."

How much to tell her, and whoever else had shifted to channel 20 and was listening in? Not much, I decided. "I am heading out to Flash of Beauty, and from there to the crime scene at Spanish Camp for some follow-up. I thought I should let someone know."

"Uh . . . okay, Teddy," Pamela stammered. She had to wonder why I was calling in. Normally, I did not report my patrol position or destination to her or anyone else. But she did not question it, instead asking, "Is there anything I can do for you?"

Asking Pamela to call Rollie Stoutt or even Deputy Commissioner Lane crossed my mind, but I rejected the idea. They would require more explanation and would probably order a delay in the arrest until they arrived. I needed to do this on my own.

"Nothing, thanks. Just reporting in." It was almost four o'clock, Pamela's usual quitting time. "I'll see you tomorrow. Out."

Ten minutes later I drove the Land Rover in low gear up the dune rise toward Flash of Beauty. Before the last curve, I stopped, killed the engine, and got out. The fresh east breeze ruffled the foliage and, maybe, just maybe, had covered the sound of the engine on the approach. Parting the sea grape branches, I was able to see the entire parking area. There was no white Mitsubishi nor any other vehicle. There was no sign of Cat or anyone else. The parking area sand was devoid of any recent vehicle tracks. Cat had not been here today.

She was somewhere on the island. I thought I could leave and probably locate her. After all, there were only so many roads and so many places to hide. But if she stayed ahead of me, or if I guessed wrong at one of the few intersections, she might avoid me. She had to have only one destination, Spanish Camp, so she had to come to Flash of Beauty. The only other way to reach the Camp of the Great Admiral was a winding cow and goat path from the east side of The Settlement. I had been on the path once, as a teen, and it was a hard, hot, dry two-mile walk through the interior I never repeated. Except for the occasional feral cow, nothing and no one used the path now. Cat was probably not even aware it existed, and if she was, there was no reason for her to choose it over the easier route that began at Flash of Beauty.

I decided to wait for Cat rather than driving out to try to find her. The next question was whether to wait at Flash of Beauty or to trek out to Spanish Camp. Wanting to leave nothing to chance, I decided to walk the beach to Spanish Camp. After all, I would look like a fool if she did walk in and out by the cow path and I missed her. And I was tired of looking like a fool. It seemed like I had spent the last six months at it.

There was just enough room to fit the Land Rover out of view on the far side of the old restaurant. I squeezed into the spot, the scrub thorn scraping finger-on-a-chalkboard against the fender and driver's-side door. To get out, I had to crawl out the passenger window. Looking back, I saw that the building and the low bushes completely obscured the car from the road and the parking lot. Brushing out the tire tracks with a sea grape branch finished the concealment.

I backed toward the water, erasing my footprints with the branch as I went. At the surf line, I discarded the branch and turned my steps toward Spanish Camp. The heat of the day was gone. The low angle of the afternoon sun backlit the beryl-blue waters of Table Bay, revealing a school of tarpon cruising for an evening meal. A pair of frigate birds squabbled with a gull in midair, finally forcing the gull to drop the sprat it carried in its mouth. One of the frigates plucked the fish from the sky before it hit the water. It had been years since I had simply walked the beach for pleasure. This walk would have been enjoyable if not for the confrontation certain to take place in the minutes or hours ahead.

After twenty minutes, I angled up the beach to the crest of the dune. Kneeling among the gray leaves of the stubby succulent plants for cover, I scanned the open area of Spanish Camp for signs of life. A chunky land crab, orphaned from the horde that had feasted on the remains of John Ippolito, marched across the open pan. A dozen flamingoes foraged in the shallows of the salt pond. There was no human movement.

I picked my way along a narrow trail through the scrub, emerging into the clearing where Ippolito had spent his last days searching for Brooks's ill-gotten cache. The elements had taken their toll, slowly expunging the traces of Ippolito's quest and his brutal end. The backpacker tent had been torn from its moorings and was now a faded sheaf of plastic pushed against the stump of a manchineel tree. Scraps of POLICE

LINE—DO NOT CROSS tape clung to a bush here and a tree there but no longer pretended to be a perimeter for the site. De White Rasta's "graves" had continued to fill through collapse and erosion, their attendant mounds of excavated material reduced to gentle humps as likely created by nature as by the hand of man. All human footprints were erased, replaced by the purposeful wakes of hermit crabs, each a set of tiny imprints straddling a deeper rut made by the purloined dwelling they each carried on their back.

Cat had not been here today. The impassive sand and the undisturbed silence told me that. But she would visit today in the short time before the sun set. I knew she would. I had only to wait.

Walking along the verge of the sand basin, I sought a break in the wall of sea grape, cactus, and scrub thorn. A step or two down a side path would allow me to see the entire area while remaining hidden from anyone approaching over the dune. At the southwest edge of the clearing, a gap in the underbrush opened diagonally onto a track, likely the terminal end of the cow path that started a couple of miles away at The Settlement. I stepped in and settled down to wait.

A half hour passed. A blinking anole, skin transmuted near-white to blend with the sand, shuffled in the dead leaves beside me. Otherwise, nothing moved. Unseen beyond the dune, swells pounded the outer reef, sounding of distant thunder. Otherwise, there was no sound.

The anxiety of waiting began, first small and mere annoyance, then prominent against the stillness. It was the anxiety of a mediocre cop, brimming with doubt and impatience, lacking confidence in the judgment and, really, the intuition that had brought him to wait in this place for the criminal he sought. A good cop might have anxiety, but only momentarily, soon to be overridden by good-cop confidence, I told myself. A good cop not only made the right choices, he instinctively knew those choices were right, even in the face of doubt.

I resisted the urge to move. More minutes passed. More doubt visited my lonely outpost.

Then there was a heavy rustling in the sea grapes behind me.

Chapter Thirty

The sound moved closer and became the steady swish of someone brushing against the undergrowth as they walked the cow path. I judged the source to be about half a cricket pitch away when the sound stopped. I waited. A minute, two minutes, then five. Silence.

No longer patient, I moved along the path. Stealth was easy. A light foot on the sand is completely noiseless. By avoiding the dry foliage bordering the trail, my approach was inaudible to whoever had been moving toward me.

The path took a sharp angle around a break in a tumbled coral wall, a field boundary left over from the days when Anegada's lifeblood was agriculture. I stepped around and into a bower of frangipani and manchineel trees. The entire space was no larger than old Ned Wheatley's one-room house in The Settlement.

On the other side of the little grove, a cow lifted her head to stare at me with languid eyes. She had been drinking from a pool shrouded by the trees. Water trickled from her hairy chin. Disturbed, but only somewhat, by my sudden appearance, she took three deliberate steps and disappeared down the far end of the path. The noise of her departure matched the rustling I had heard earlier. I realized I had, quite literally, been on a wild cow chase. Just more quality police work, being drawn from my stakeout by a cow.

I walked over to the pool. It was a pleasant spot, dappled with shade from the squat trees. Animals visited here regularly; the ground was a kaleidoscope of hoof and claw prints. Two sides of the pool were bordered by slabs of limestone. The water was cool to the touch and fresh to the taste. This might have been one of the limestone sinks where Columbus's shore party had refilled their water casks five centuries ago.

Peering into the water, I could make out shelves of rock angling away into the depths. The bottom of the well was not discernible. I was about to double back to my stakeout when the memory of words I had read twice in the past week struck me.

He was wet from head to foot.

It was the very first line Anthony Wedderburn had been able to decipher from the notebook found in Kelliher/Ippolito's possessions. I had read the words again just hours ago in Anthony's almost-complete decoding. Neville Wells had not understood why Nigel Brooks had returned from Spanish Camp on that fateful night in 1970 "wet from head to foot" with freshwater. John Ippolito had not either, spending his last days at the Camp of the Great Admiral digging when he should have been doing something else.

He should have been diving.

I could have returned to my stakeout location and waited to capture Cat Wells. There would have been ample opportunity to explore the pool on another day. Who knows, an interrogation of Cat at RVIPF headquarters might have confirmed her involvement and motive, and made it easy to persuade Deputy Commissioner Lane to order divers to search the pool for Nigel Brooks's shagreen bag and its mysterious contents. Waiting would have been the prudent course of action. But in the end I succumbed to the same fever, the same yearning, the same quest for a treasure trove that had impelled inhabitants of the Caribbean since the days of the buccaneers.

I kicked off my sandals and shed my uniform shirt. The slide from the limestone shelf into the algid water took my breath for a moment. There was just enough room for me to scissor and dive.

A body length below the surface, color faded to a leaden gray-green but the water remained air-clear. I twisted in a tight circle and saw that the mouth of the sink was lined with broken rock shelves and cavities. Light failed to reach the rearmost confines of these ledges and hollows. I reached in up to my shoulder in the one nearest me.

A murky cloud of silt puffed from the crevice I had probed. Leaves and bits of vegetation falling into the sink from above had decomposed where they landed, undisturbed for years. The slightest movement caused this detritus to billow up from where it lay. I reached into another shelf as visibility in the immediate area went to zero. My hand touched limestone shards and soupy plant matter but nothing else.

Lungs bursting, I surfaced. Treading water, I hyperventilated as I do when diving for conch. After three minutes of forcing extra oxygen into my bloodstream, I plunged again, deeper this time, hoping to work from the bottom of the sink upward to keep the clouds of silt below as I searched the ledges. Now one side of the pool was clouded, as was the water below my waist, as I pulled upright to work along the rock walls. Nothing man-made met my grasp, and I rose to the surface for a rest and another lungful of air.

I made another dive and then two others with no success. I began to doubt. Even if I was correct and Brooks had hidden his bag in a limestone sink, it did not necessarily have to be *this* limestone sink. There were many wells and sinks dotting Anegada; exploring the bush near Spanish Camp would probably reveal a dozen wells, potholes, and sinks of various sizes.

I was tiring, and when I next surfaced, I kicked over onto my back to float and rest. The sun was no longer visible overhead and the light had a late-day tinge, deep purple on the eastern horizon. I told myself I would make two more dives and call it a day. Then, with luck, I could still make it back to Flash of Beauty before full dark. It would mean trying to find Cat somewhere on the island in the dark. I expected it would mean that I would not find her.

Diving down into the roiled pool had become diving blind. The final searches would be by touch alone. My knuckles and fingertips were raw and sore, and by the time I ascended from the next-to-last dive, my ego was bruised as well. Treading water and faint from holding my breath, I thought I had failed again.

The light overhead was pallid. The sun was almost at the western horizon. I rolled and kicked down, closing my eyes to keep out the particles floating everywhere in the water. At the front of a ledge, my hand fell upon something long and smooth. Seizing the object in my right hand, I felt further back into the gelatinous mud with my left. I touched something solid but yielding, certainly man-made. Sliding my hand further along, I gripped an asymmetry in its smooth surface. Both hands full and lungs empty, I rose toward the fading light above.

Chapter Thirty-One

Breaking through the water's surface, I flung both arms onto the rock shelf beside the well. The prizes from the dive revealed themselves. In my right hand was a cow femur, black with age and immediately discarded. My left hand was closed around the handles of a miraculously well-preserved leather bag. The leather was dimpled and gray, retaining the color and texture of the sharkskin from which it had been made. The bag was heavy for its size, the contents lumpy inside.

Pulling myself onto the rock, I sat with my feet and legs in the water and the bag on my lap. My heart raced, as much from excitement as from the repeated dives into the pool. You have Nigel Brooks's treasure in your hand, the voice inside my head said. I willed myself to be calm and waited for my breathing to slow.

I upended the bag, spilling its contents onto the limestone

beside me. A dozen plastic baggies, turned opaque from immersion but intact, sat piled beside my right hip. All were tied with what had been a paper-and-wire twist tie, the paper now disintegrated and the wire a lacy tangle of rust that crumbled at my touch. I emptied the first baggie into my palm.

The last rays of the sun were captured and then cast back from the opulent cascade that rolled into my hand. Round, square, rectangular, even triangular nodes of faceted green overflowed onto the ground. Large as tern eggs, small as crabs' eyes, and every size in between, burnished and flashing the full spectrum of green, the green of spring grass, of the pale shallows of the flats, of the ominous edge of a thunderhead, of the black-green depths beyond the boundary of the reef, of Cat Wells's teasing eyes. Emeralds. A half pound of stones in the baggie I opened, and the next, and the next. Emeralds enough to decorate the delicate lobes of a thousand princesses' ears, grace the décolletage of a decade's worth of debutantes, and still have enough to appease a hundred petulant mistresses.

I was giddy, emptying baggie after baggie onto the flat rock until I seemed seated at the edge of an emerald beach, the gems as numerous as grains of sand, suitable not for constructing castles of sand, but real castles, mansions, manors, villas, estates. I laughed aloud and ran my fingers through the hoard. I was rich.

And then I was not. I stopped laughing. This treasure belonged to me no more than it did to Nigel Brooks. It belonged to the people of Anegada, to the people of the BVI, and it had been taken from them. The theft that had paid for this trove had set back my island for decades. My country's very dreams had been traded for these jewels. They were stolen goods. And I was a policeman. I pulled on my uniform shirt, as much as a reminder of this as to ward off the cool of the evening air.

I carefully picked up the gems, refilling each baggie until all but the last had been repacked with its cargo. Fearing to move lest I knock loose emeralds back into the well, I scanned the ground where I sat, picking up the stones with my right hand while I held my finds in my left. The sun was flush against the horizon. I worried about locating all the emeralds before dark.

Concentrating on the task at hand, I was unaware of a person approaching until a long shadow fell across the emeralds scattered before me. I looked up to see a figure, female but otherwise unidentifiable, silhouetted against the setting sun. From there events took on a surreal quality, proceeding in slow motion, laden with disbelief.

The arm of the figure rose toward me. A flat slap of sound split the silence and dissipated into the open country. An unseen force punched me to the ground. The emeralds in my hand took flight, hesitated at their apogee, and pattered into the pool with a sound of raindrops. I felt as if someone were sitting on my chest. Warm liquid spread along the ground beneath my shoulders and back. My head rolled to face west. Two points of light rode low in the violet sky. Mars and Venus, I realized.

Then darkness fell.

Chapter Thirty-Two

"Wake up!"

The voice was insistent but buried, muffled, calling from beneath a pile of pillows or the bottom of one of the open graves at Spanish Camp.

The kick in my ribs was more immediate. I heard a groan and realized it was me.

"Wake up, you cheating bastard. You don't die until I say you die." The voice rose slowly from its buried place until it hovered over me. "Wake up, whoremonger."

Another kick. I inhaled sharply. Pain flooded in, a flaming poker in the right side of my chest. A dull timpani beat agony at the back of my skull. The kick was mere icing on the cake.

A savage, angry third kick. My eyes flew open. Icilda stood over me, her face a mask of rage. Her clothing was damp with sweat. Her scent carried an animal quality, heavy and primal. She spat in my face.

I tried to roll upright but my legs, still dangling in the water of the sink, provided no firm purchase. All I managed was a feeble flop.

Icilda laughed at my effort, a tuneless, empty laugh, like she knew she should laugh and wanted to stick to the script but knew it was bad acting.

"You're a big man now, aren't you, Teddy? Flopping like a beached mullet and bleeding out your pathetic little life onto the sand. You disgust me, cheating on me with that whore of Babylon. Like I didn't know it. I knew it from the start, you sorry excuse for a man. You thought you were so clever. Well, the last laugh is mine. I'm going to enjoy watching while you bleed and squirm."

The odor of cordite filtered through the waves of pain. Only then did it register that I had been shot. That my wife, Icilda, had shot me. I tilted my head and saw the source of the cordite smell in her hand, my own RVIPF Webley. She was close enough that I made a weak effort to grab it, which she parried with a jabbing kick directly into my chest wound. Pain seared through my body. I vomited and she laughed. This time the laughter was genuine.

"That's right, Teddy, your own gun," she said, sighting down the barrel at my forehead. "Be careful or I might have to do to you what I did to Ippolito before you get the full explanation." She paused and the realization must have shown in my eyes. "Right again, Teddy. Your gun killed Ippolito.

Easy as can be, just get the safe combination from your wallet, visit your office after hours while you were chasing around with that hussy, do what needed to be done, and put it back in the safe after my shift at the Reef."

Suddenly she seemed agitated and braced as if ready to shoot. I had to buy time. I did the only thing I could think to do. I croaked out, "Why?'

"Why what, Teddy?" Icilda took a mental step back. "Why did I kill Ippolito? Or why am I going to kill you, is that your question? Same answer to both, I suppose. And I did promise you an explanation before I finish up the happy task of killing you.

"The answer to your question is—to get myself out of this hellhole, that's why. To have a life, a real life. I know you think I have it wonderful here and I have for all these years. Living in that glorified shack. Up half the night waiting tables at the Reef, hoping some fat Kraut is gonna leave me a two-dollar tip. Changing every diaper that was ever messed by our two kids without a finger lifted by you. Home alone in an empty bed while you were out playing slap-ass with that jezebel. The only excitement what's on TV or happening at the church. Oh, yeah, the church, with the Right Reverend Lloyd rubbing up against me and whispering in my ear, trying to convince hisself he's not a faggot. Yeah, I got it good, Teddy. I thought I was stuck here forever until Poppa was on his deathbed.

"Poppa told me then about working for Nigel Brooks and how he took Brooks on his boat ride out of Anegada when he made his escape. He told me about Brooks's making his detour to Spanish Camp and leaving a bag there. Poppa thought whatever was in the bag was part of Brooks's take from his scam. He thought Brooks buried it. He and one of Brooks's old helicopter pilots, John Ippolito, got hooked up five years ago after they stumbled onto one another, both of them digging up Spanish Camp. Ippolito had an alias and a cover ID as Paul Kelliher because he thought he was wanted in the BVI for abetting Brooks's escape. Poppa and Ippolito threw in together and dug for years, using metal detectors and just plain guessing about the location of the bag left by Brooks.

"Poppa and Ippolito dug up and reburied most of the area behind the dune from Table Bay to the East End. When he took sick, Poppa couldn't dig anymore and Ippolito went on without him. Poppa told me all about it the day before he died. He wanted me to have you pick up with Ippolito where he had left off.

"I thought about it, for a few days. I thought about it in the church at Poppa's funeral, about finding all that money and how it could get me off this godforsaken rock forever. I thought about how I'd never have to wait another table or wash another load of clothes again.

"And you just didn't figure into those plans, Teddy. Not you who came home from a day of work smelling of fish and came to my bed at night smelling the same way. Not you who grunted at me over the favorite meal I fixed for you and thought it passed for brilliant conversation. Not you who thought wham-bam-thank-you-ma'am twice a year took care of my romantic needs. No, I decided my new start would be without you.

"I decided to see the world, first class all the way. I decided I would take lovers on every continent and their very existence would be for the purpose of satisfying *me*. No more whining kids, no more church as social life, no more wasting my days away out here on the backside of nowhere. When Ippolito and I found Brooks's bag of gold or diamonds or whatever it was, we would split it and I would be gone before you knew what happened. I cried when I decided, tears of happiness, tears of joy at my upcoming liberation from it all, right there at Poppa's funeral. Everyone thought I was grieving.

"When I first approached Ippolito, he pretended not to know what I was talking about. He even disavowed his real name. I finally told him Poppa had given me a map before he died. The fool caved right in. Didn't he think if Poppa had a map he would have used it already? He was desperate, or maybe crazy from all those years out digging in the sun, but we made a deal. We would go fifty-fifty on anything we found. He would dig. My contribution would be the map and keeping him in food and supplies.

"I had to come up with a map, so I sat down at the kitchen table and drew one on a legal pad. X marks the spot and everything. He was easy to fool; he wanted to believe so badly. I just wanted to keep him digging, 'cause Poppa said he thought they were finally in the right area. I had to make the map look old so I put it in the oven. Two hundred degrees for two hours and it came out looking like it was forty years old. Best baking I ever did.

"Ippolito bought it, hook, line, and sinker. He dug and dug. I snuck food and water out to him. It wasn't hard 'cause you were never home anyway.

"Six months into our partnership and it looked like all I got was another mouth to feed. I figured sooner or later you would notice the increase in the food budget, even though I was taking him stolen leftovers from the Reef half the time. I was almost ready to call it quits when Ippolito said he had been contacted by his dead pilot buddy's kid. She said she had a coded notebook with information about the night Brooks hid his treasure. She told him she wanted an equal share for the information.

"I wasn't enthusiastic about another person having a cut. On the other hand, right then I had fifty percent of nothing. So I said yes, and next thing I know, your little dog bitch in heat is here, flying around in her helicopter. I suppose she came to keep an eye on her investment but pretty soon she took over the supply run. And she needed to find some amusement and you, you lagga head, you jump into her pants. Like I didn't know. She told me right away and we had a good laugh about how we were keeping a full-time watch on the whole Anegada po-lice force.

"Then one day Ippolito told me he was going to cut me out. Told me my map was no good, that he would get better clues from the notebook, which he and your whore never would let me see. I told him he couldn't do that to me and he said,

'Why, what you going to do about it?' and laughed at me. So the next evening I went to your office safe and got the gun, to scare him.

"When I got to Ippolito's camp, we had a shouting match and he pushed me down on the sand. I had the gun in my bag and I pulled it out and pointed it right at his face. He said he was tired of trouble with the help and reached for the gun. I shot him dead, left the scum right where he dropped, and put the gun back in the safe after my late shift at the Reef that night.

"After giving Ippolito the reward for his loyalty, I tried to figure how to get my hands on the clue notebook. Next thing I know, you practically drop it in my hands, giving it to that ganja-toking vagrant White Rasta to decode. And right at church where I could keep an eye on him till he was about done. Too bad I had to whack him to get the book, but he never seemed to let the damn thing out of his sight. Anyway, he never saw me, never saw it coming. And the decoding didn't do much good once I got it. It was just a bunch of nonsense about the Camp of the Great Admiral and running around in the moonlight.

"When all those drug agents came to the island, I figured I better lie low for a while and I did. Then that little bitch of yours came poking around out here, looking to find Brooks's stash all for herself. She spent most of this week here, while you were off chasing your tail. I heard her helicopter come in this afternoon and then the next thing is you calling Pamela Pickering to say you are coming out here.

"I figure the two of you wouldn't come way out here to fuck when you already had so many other convenient locations for it around the island. The only reason to come here was for the treasure, and then you and she would fly out and disappear. So I decided to visit the police station safe again and take a sunset stroll. I was hoping to catch you both, but all I got was you. Lucky how you found Brooks's little package and ended up parked right in my path.

"So that's not only the 'why' but the 'how,' Teddy. Now you get your reward and I get mine. I'll get the kids off to school tomorrow morning, kiss them good-bye, and tell them to go to Sidney and Lily's house after school, just like when we're both working. They'll be fine with their grandparents, probably better off than having a cheating, lowlife daddy and a miserable mother. I'll be on the *Bomba Charger* by eight, in San Juan by ten, and on my way to Europe or South America by noon, just me and my faithful companion, that pile of emeralds you were so good to gather for me. By the time your exalted RVIPF sorts out what happened, I'll be someone else, in a place far, far away. And you'll still be dead, you whore-chasing, ungrateful bastard."

As Icilda finished her rant, the world became distant and fuzzy at the edges. I tried to move again and only succeeded in turning my head to the side. Blood dampened my cheek and flowed in a dark rivulet to stain the waters of the pool. Another kick from my once-meek, churchgoing wife refocused my attention on her and the Webley. The eternal eye of the barrel stared back at me, quaking slightly as tension was applied to the trigger.

In a voice overflowing with anger, Icilda said, "Good-bye, Teddy. I'll see you in hell."

I was far along the shadowy tunnel toward unconsciousness when I heard a sound, followed by the vague recognition that the sound was a pistol being fired.

Chapter Thirty-Three

"Come on, Teddy, stay with me. Breathe, breathe!" The voice was commanding and clear. My lungs obeyed and took in air, albeit with a wet gurgle on the right side. Pain marched in on the heels of consciousness.

"That's it, Teddy, keep breathing, stay with me." My shirt was torn from my body by strong hands. A sudden pressure below my right shoulder became the focus of the pain. I realized it was a cloth or bandage being pressed against me.

"Come on, Teddy, don't give up."

I opened my eyes. At first I made out nothing in the day's last light. Concentrating, I was able to materialize a form, then a face, and finally a pair of assured green eyes above me.

"That's it, lover. Wake up and stay with me. You're not going to die if I can help it," Cat Wells said in a calm voice, soothing, but strong. She willed me to consciousness through that voice, and I grasped, clawed, clung to it as if it were a rope tossed to a drowning man.

I came fully to the world and the pain rose to full flood, radiating from my chest to every corner of my being.

"You've been shot, Teddy, and you have a chest wound," Cat said.

Of course, of course, I remembered I had been shot. Icilda shot me, with my own Webley. Icilda! I struggled to speak. No words came, held down, driven deep inside my body by the weight on my chest.

My eyes sought the cause of the weight and found Cat's upper arm above the pressure point. I could not lower my vision enough to see the arm's end, but Cat followed my gaze.

"The weight you feel is me, Teddy, applying pressure to your wound to stop the bleeding. Looks like I finally found a way to get rid of that ratty uniform shirt of yours, using it as a bandage," she said lightly, trying to keep me from concern.

I managed a wheezing grunt in acknowledgment. She pressed the wound firmly and said nothing more. I looked closely at her. She wore a once-crisply-pressed VI Birds pilot's shirt, now damp with sweat and unbuttoned down the front. She had a white tank top beneath and a shoulder holster which carried a Smith & Wesson .38, butt forward. At the same moment I saw the gun, the stink of cordite filled my nostrils for the second time in minutes.

Cat peeled off her outer shirt, switching hands to keep pressure on the wound. She reached to her belt and came away with a folding knife, which she effortlessly flicked open with one hand.

“Teddy, can you move your hands? Try,” Cat urged.

I accomplished a weak wave of my right.

“Okay, I’m putting your hand on the wound and I want you to press as hard as you can.”

Cat jammed my right hand against the crude compress she had made with my shirt. This resulted in a disturbing sensation of wet and warm. I was now fully aware and tried not to panic.

Cat sliced her pilot’s shirt into long strips and tied them end to end. She half-rolled me to the left to place the strips beneath me, sending a constellation of agony through me. The resulting scream was that of a wounded beast, primal and afraid. Sweat beaded my forehead and gathered in runnels to the corners of my mouth.

Cat finished binding my wound, gingerly cinching the strips to hold the folded shirt tight against my oozing chest. I felt light-headed and thirsty. Between these two conditions and my general weakness, I still could not speak. Cat must have known that shock and blood loss called for hydration and brought water from the pool to me in cupped hands, drizzling it slowly onto my parched lips.

“Lover, we have to turn you onto your right side to help you breathe and to make sure fluid doesn’t drain into your uninjured lung and drown you. I’ll try to make it as quick as

I can." She turned me before there was time for me to think about it. Incandescent pain gave way to merciful oblivion.

"You went out for a minute, lover," Cat said when I struggled awake. "Sorry about the pain but it had to be done. You can rest easy now."

I still lay on the limestone shelf where I had fallen when Icilda shot me. That event seemed long ago but full darkness had yet to arrive. Breathing seemed easier. I saw a shape in the dim light, three yards away. It was Icilda, with her legs twisted at impossible angles. Her eyes stared directly at me but showed no recognition. The lower part of her jaw had been shot away by the .38 slug on its way to making a gaping wound in what had once been her throat. The Webley rested an arm's length away from her outstretched fingers.

Cat took a bandana from her trouser pocket and covered Icilda's face. "I had to do it, Teddy. She was going to kill you," Cat said, part in apology, part in explanation.

I tried to focus, tried to understand, tried to put it all together. Thoughts drifted and raced but I was unable to make sense of any of it.

Cat sat down beside me and wiped my brow. Her scent cascaded over me, the raw sexuality redolent even in this most unsexual of moments. She picked up the shagreen bag and deliberately placed the baggies of emeralds, one after another, inside. Then she bent and kissed me on the forehead.

"We had some good times together, didn't we, lover?" Cat murmured. Then, not expecting or wanting an answer, she rose to her feet.

"Good luck, Teddy," she said, tossing the words over her shoulder as she stepped down the path toward Spanish Camp and the beach beyond, the shagreen bag and its cargo of emeralds dangling from her right hand.

Chapter Thirty-Four

I felt warm life leaking steadily from my chest. I tried to move, thrashed weakly, and abraded my knees and elbows on the sharp edges of the few emeralds that remained scattered beneath me. The darkness of the tropics descended utterly and completely. With no clouds above, a coolness came over the land and chilled me to the core. The voice inside me said, This is what it's like to die. Twilight sleep without dreams came.

My waking was a surprise. I had consigned myself to oblivion, not as a mindful decision, but rather by acceptance that it was happening and I had no say in the matter. The thump of cattle hooves on the limestone where I lay had interrupted my passage to eternity. A half dozen of the creatures ranged around the pool, drinking. An alabaster half moon showed directly overhead, turning cows, water, and sand into shades of silver and steel. I moved my head. The cows, who had convinced themselves that I was just an inanimate part of the landscape, bolted into the sea grapes, leaving me alone in the moonlight.

A slow understanding that I had a choice to make worked its way to me through the haze of shock and injury. I could stay where I was and be found in a day or a week, dead and picked apart by crabs like John Ippolito. Or I could muster whatever strength remained in me and try to get out of this place and back to the world.

Rolling to my knees caused a surge of vertigo. I lowered my head and willed the blood to flow there. Nearly blacking out, I stayed still until my vision cleared, facing down at the limestone. There my dried blood appeared gray in the moonlight. In the blood was a smattering of emeralds, sparking ice green even in the monochromatic light. I ignored them. They were no good to me now.

I shuffled on my knees to the edge of the pool and bent to drink from the cool water. It helped, a little. I tried to stand, without success. All energy had departed my body; my best effort produced only a crawl.

So I crawled along the path toward Spanish Camp, crawled for long hours as the moon dropped in the western sky. By the time I reached the place where John Ippolito had died, the lowering moon cast leaden shadows against the excavations there, a ghostly hillock of barren sand beside each one.

I told myself I would rest awhile but the truth was that I could not go on. I slept, or passed out, I know not which.

Dreams of the mutilated Ippolito and of Icilda's lifeless eyes marred any rest I got. Or perhaps they were not dreams but the visitation of ghosts, duppies in that place of death. That night I traveled the dune and the salt pan with them, my fitful dozing an approach and retreat from the boundary between life and the grave. But my spirit, soul, or being—call it what you may—refused the duppies' invitation.

The first light of day brought me back from my sojourn with the dead. I clawed to the crest of the dune in time to see the sun rise from the fathomless waters of the Anegada Trench.

With the sun came a powerful heat, as the trade winds had not yet begun. With the heat came a powerful thirst. It had been twelve hours since I had drunk from the pool. Loss of blood had depleted my fluids and the broiling dawn seemed determined to finish the job. I was confronted with a choice between bad and worse: either return to the pool or continue the mile or more up the beach to Flash of Beauty. Going on presented a better chance of being found but no prospect of water. Going back might mean I would be well hydrated when I died. At the rate I was able to travel, Flash of Beauty would take all day, exposed to the sun and still bleeding.

This sounds as if options were weighed and a rational decision was made. In truth, after a moment's hesitation, I plunged down the dune face, not really cognizant of making a choice. Going forward was simply the only thing my reeling mind could comprehend and the only thing it could direct my broken body to do.

The foot-tall succulents at the base of the dune provided shade enough for a crawling man. I lingered there, breathing heavily, sweat and blood mingling on my chest. I passed out again and only roused at midmorning.

The sand was firmest at the tide line, so that is where I crawled. The first half an hour of movement required half an hour of rest, immobile and baking on the exposed shore. The next half hour required an hour's halt to recover. The next, two hours. I swam through a sea of sand, limbs too weak to raise my body above the parching grains. The sun moved overhead, burning my back and neck, adding another stratum of torment.

By midafternoon, I had reached the eastern end of Table Bay. The seep of blood from my chest wound had stopped, if only because all liquid seemed to have congealed and been drawn from my body. I was a husk, dry as the sand I crawled on. Visions danced before me in the dazzling light, conch shells on human legs, feral cows speaking with the same Rasta patois as Anthony Wedderburn, tarpon and bonefish swimming facilely through the dunes. In a moment of clarity, I understood that I would not reach Flash of Beauty for hours, perhaps not for another day, at the pace I traveled.

My mouth was a cave filled with dust. In my fevered brain, the sea was an infinite chalice of quenching aquamarine nectar, mere steps away. One small drink cannot hurt, I told myself. A small drink might save me. I turned my body toward the waves and pushed with arms and legs. And did not move. Again I made the effort and again there was no movement.

My cheek pressed into the hot sand, my eyes level an inch above its surface. Far to seaward, breakers, come from Africa, roared white against Horseshoe Reef. A shadow crossed the near ground and then merged with its source, a herring gull, when the bird alighted a few feet from my head. Its hungry obsidian eye betrayed no fear, though I was a hundred times the bird's size. I tried to shoo the thing. My body did not answer. I could not twitch a finger.

The black eye stared at mine, searching. Another shadow heralded another gull. Then more and more gathered. The first bird inclined its head, took a step toward me, waited, and then hopped forward quickly. His compatriots crowded to follow. I felt the brush of feathers against my arm.

I used the last of my strength to close my eyes.

Chapter Thirty-Five

The chittering call of a bananaquit drifted through my hazy consciousness. It began far away and moved closer and closer, enticing but not insistent, until I opened my eyes. Buoyant motes of dust moved across the dark-light pattern of sun filtered by a venetian blind. It was a friendly sun, warm and cheery, containing no threat of desiccation and death. There was no pain, no thirst, no fear in this place, only the clement glow of safety and repose.

The radiant brume of my awakening cleared enough for me to remember the state of affairs when I had closed my eyes. How I had gone from that situation to this was a mystery my unfocused mind sought to solve. I had moved from peril to safety, from pain to comfort, with no effort other than surrendering to fate. There could be only one explanation. I decided I was dead.

No sooner had I reached this conclusion than a vaguely familiar voice disabused me of it.

"Constable Creque, I see you are back with us. You've had a bit of a tough go but you are safe and in good hands now."

The voice was solicitous and reassuring. Maybe that was why it took a moment to place it. The last time I had heard it, the voice and its owner were all business. But the Abaco accent was unmistakable.

Nurse Rowell was standing next to the soft bed where I lay. She placed a gentle hand on my shoulder when I tried to get up.

"You have been shot," she said, her voice oil smoothing troubled waters. "You are in the Intensive Care Unit of Peebles Hospital in Road Town. You must be still. You have a tube down your throat to help you breathe. You have been unconscious for three days since you were brought in from Anegada."

Three days! Nurse Rowell saw the panic in my eyes. Three days was more than enough time for Cat to get away with the emeralds. I tried to gesture for something to write on. My left arm was restrained to the point of immobility; my right was entangled in tubes and monitor cords.

"Easy, Constable, no need to become agitated. I'll give you something to write on but you must promise to be still." Nurse Rowell's calm eyes locked on mine. I nodded. She produced a small notepad and pen from the pocket of her pristine white uniform.

"STOP WELLS," I wrote. The handwriting wobbled and dipped through the lines on the notepad.

Nurse Rowell watched me scratch out the words and said, "She has been stopped, Constable, with a fortune in emeralds in her possession. It is all over the newspapers, how you solved the Anegada murder and were shot after recovering the money that had been embezzled by Nigel Brooks. I daresay you are the first national hero we have had the pleasure of treating here at Peebles. Now be still and relax. Your Deputy Commissioner Lane has asked to be contacted as soon as you regained consciousness. I will go call him now. I'm sure he will explain it all in detail to you." Nurse Rowell padded noiselessly from the room.

A short time later a brisk young doctor wearing a saffron *pagri* entered the room with Nurse Rowell. "I am Dr. Patel, your attending physician. Nurse Rowell says you have been pretty chipper, so we are going to remove the tube in your throat and see how you do breathing on your own. When we begin to remove the tube, just open your throat and try not to cough."

Thirty seconds later, the irritation of the tube was gone, replaced by a roaring sore throat that seemed to extend from the back of my tongue to the pit of my stomach. Nurse Rowell fed me soothing ice chips, one at a time. I savored each one, remembering my thirsting crawl along the beach to Table Bay three days before.

Nurse Rowell had gone for more ice when the ramrod-straight figure of Deputy Commissioner Howard T. Lane appeared in the doorway. He hesitated for a moment before entering.

"Special Constable Creque, you had us all worried. How are you feeling?" He was a policeman through and through; even the DC's bluff inquiry after my health had a note of interrogation in it.

My effort to answer was a rasping, incoherent gurgle. Nurse Rowell returned at that moment and fixed a laser glare on the DC, which was returned in kind. It crossed my mind that they might come to blows.

"Constable Creque has just had his breathing tube removed and speaking will be painful and difficult for him until the irritation from the tube has healed," she said.

"I see," the DC said, sheepish for the first time in memory. "Perhaps I should come back later."

I shook my head wildly, drawing both the DC's and Nurse Rowell's attention.

"The constable wrote a note. It said, 'STOP WELLS.' I told him you had already detained Ms. Wells and would explain further when you arrived. I don't think the constable will rest peacefully until he has an explanation of what occurred. Perhaps you could provide the explanation without making him speak. It would aid his recovery." Nurse Rowell arched an eyebrow by way of inquiry.

The eyebrow froze the DC for a moment. Then he gruffly cleared his throat, said, "Very well," and seated himself in a metal folding chair Nurse Rowell pulled down from a wall hook behind the door.

"Not too much excitement, Deputy Commissioner. He may be your special constable but right now he is *my* patient and

I will permit nothing that upsets him," she said. The DC nodded his agreement and Nurse Rowell retired from the room.

"To begin, Special Constable, let me address your concern about apprehending Mary Catherine Wells," the deputy commissioner said. "We have Ms. Wells in custody, held in Her Majesty's Prison while the senior crown counsel prepares charges against her. Her arrest is the end result of several very busy days set in motion by you, and I think it would be best to go back to the beginning so you have a complete picture.

"Four days ago, the administrator for Anegada arrived at work to find your two children waiting for her on the doorstep of the administration building." Catching my expression, the DC halted.

"Don't worry, Constable, they are safe with their grandmother and grandfather."

He continued. "Your children were concerned that neither you nor your wife had been home during the previous night. Ms. Pickering contacted your parents to arrange for the care of your children. She also recalled that you had informed her on the previous afternoon that you were going to the area of Spanish Camp as a part of your investigation of the murder that had taken place there. She did not, however, contact RVIPF headquarters concerning your disappearance. As she later explained it, she did not do so because she feared your activities might further endanger your job with the RVIPF, which she was convinced was already hanging by the thinnest of threads. Instead, she put out a call for the organization of a search for you on the CB radio. By noon, every household in Anegada had responded, with nearly all able-bodied residents scouring the island from one end to the other trying to locate you and your wife.

"Ms. Pickering herself started for Flash of Beauty. On her way, she passed the airport and caught sight of a VI Birds helicopter parked in the aircraft taxi area.

"Because she had not heard the helicopter arrive that day, and because VI Birds never leaves its aircraft on Anegada overnight, she investigated and found the cockpit unlocked and the engine compartment open. As she described it to me, when she looked inside the open engine hatch, it appeared 'some crazy man took an ax or a hammer an' bust everything he could bust inside.' I assume that individual was you?" The DC lowered his head toward me, looking for confirmation. I nodded agreement.

"I thought so. A rather unorthodox police tactic, the purposeful destruction of property, but effective in this instance."

DC Lane went on. "At that point, Ms. Pickering decided it was time to involve the RVIPF and contacted my office. At nearly the same time, the owner of VI Birds contacted Virgin Islands Search and Rescue to report that the company's helicopter was overdue and missing. Apparently the pilot, Mary Catherine Wells, had reported mechanical problems while at Lettsome airport on Beef Island the day before. She had advised VI Birds that she would see to the needed repairs at Lettsome overnight and return to St. Thomas in the morning. When the helicopter had not returned by noon and Ms. Wells had not reported in, the owner contacted the tower at

Lettsome and was told the aircraft had left the evening before, filing a flight plan to Anegada and then to San Juan. VISAR began an air/sea search and, of course, contacted the US Coast Guard and the RVIPF.

"By the time we put this all together, it was midafternoon. We dispatched the *St. Ursula* with Inspector Stoutt and ten officers to aid in the search for what we then thought were three missing persons on Anegada. The *St. Ursula* arrived shortly after the *Bomba Charger* left the Anegada government dock for its scheduled return trip to Road Town. Ms. Pickering was present to meet Inspector Stoutt and his men, and received a radio call on their arrival that two of the Anegada searchers, a Mr. Wendell George and Ms. Marie Benoit, had found you on the beach at Table Bay, unconscious and in dire need of medical attention.

"Inspector Stoutt and four officers immediately left with Ms. Pickering for Table Bay. The remaining officers met with some of the Anegada volunteers at the dock to coordinate their search efforts. During the course of this, the volunteers were informed for the first time that the search also involved locating Ms. Wells. One of the volunteers, Ms. Belle Lloyd, mentioned that she thought she saw Ms. Wells board the *Bomba Charger* that day shortly before it departed for Road Town. She described Ms. Wells as 'looking disheveled, like she had spent the night sleeping on the beach.'

"The officers radioed headquarters but by the time a patrol car reached the Road Town ferry dock, Ms. Wells had debarked and disappeared. Unsure of what exactly was taking place, and with a significant part of the manpower of the police force involved in the search on Anegada, I enlisted the help of Agent Rosenblum and his JITFS agents to locate Ms. Wells.

"Agent Rosenblum caught up with her at Lettsome airport, just as she was walking onto the tarmac to board a LIAT flight to Sint Maarten. She was calm and cooperative but insistent that she board the flight. Agent Rosenblum was able to stall her long enough for his men to pull her baggage. A loaded Smith & Wesson .38 was found in her checked bag. She had no BVI permit to possess or carry the weapon and was arrested. When her purse was searched following her arrest, a forged Netherlands passport, in the name of Edit de Weever and bearing Ms. Wells's photo, was found, together with an e-ticket confirmation number. The e-ticket was for a Copa Airlines flight that day from Sint Maarten to Buenos Aries, Argentina, by way of Panama City, Panama, with Edit de Weever listed as the passenger.

"Ms. Wells also had a carry-on bag that had passed through the metal detector at the boarding gate without incident. Inside it were found approximately five pounds of high-quality Colombian emeralds, with a retail value since estimated to be in excess of fifty million dollars."

My face must have expressed what my voice could not. The DC said, "That's right, Special Constable, fifty million dollars. I suspect my eyes bugged out just like yours when I first heard that number.

"Ms. Wells was brought to headquarters for questioning.

The Smith & Wesson was examined and determined to have been recently fired. By then, you were being brought to Peebles Hospital on the *St. Ursula* with a bullet wound in your chest. As a result, I personally conducted the questioning of Ms. Wells. When I revealed to her that you had been found critically wounded but alive, she seemed relieved. The news about you removed any hesitancy she had about responding to my questions.

"She told a story so remarkable that I actually believed it. But it would help for you to confirm it where possible. An affirmative or negative nod of the head will suffice until you have recovered and are able to prepare a full written report. Do you feel up to it?"

I did not. I gestured affirmatively anyway.

"Very well. The most important item first. Did Ms. Wells shoot you?" The DC looked intently into my eyes.

I shook my head no.

"Ms. Wells said she shot and killed your wife, Icilda, to prevent Icilda from killing you."

Yes.

"Ms. Wells says that it was Icilda who wounded you, using your own service revolver."

I slowly nodded yes.

The DC's brow furrowed. "I am sorry, Constable, that your personal . . . situation, is involved here and that your marriage has come to this."

His comment was a strange way to put it, but what could DC Lane really say? Since being shot, I had been too busy staying alive to think about it but reality registered now. Icilda was dead. Dead trying to kill me. Icilda was a murderer, cold and calculating. I was an adulterer. Our marriage was over long before the sunset confrontation at Spanish Camp. It was over years before, even before I sat at Rot Faulkner's funeral and dried her tears as she plotted to cast me, our family, and our life on Anegada aside.

I mouthed "thank you" and the DC went on.

"Ms. Wells says that she believes Icilda was responsible for the murder of Professor Paul Kelliher, who was not, in fact, a professor at all, but an individual named John Ippolito."

"Icilda confessed it to me," I rasped. My eyes teared, whether from the pain and effort of speech or the emotion rising inside me, I could not tell.

"I see," DC Lane said. "When did she make this confession to you?"

"After," was all I got out before all sound ceased to come from me.

"After what? After she wounded you?"

Yes, said the nod of my head.

"Did Icilda also confess to assaulting Anthony Wedderburn?" he asked. "Ms. Wells said she suspected Icilda had committed that crime as well."

My head bent in assent.

DC Lane changed direction. "Ms. Wells said in her statement that John Ippolito was a friend of her father and that her father had worked for Nigel Brooks on Anegada in the late nineteen sixties. She told a long story but the gist was that

Ms. Wells, Ippolito, and Icilda had information that they believed would lead them to the money Nigel Brooks had embezzled from the government of the Virgin Islands. Did you know this?"

I dipped my chin in agreement.

"How did you know this?" the DC asked, his voice a mixture of curiosity and surprise.

"Investigation," I whispered. I would have dearly loved to have had a camera to record the DC's expression when he heard that word.

"And did your investigation also lead you to the cache of emeralds that Ms. Wells had in her possession when she was arrested, Special Constable?"

I signaled a yes.

"Ms. Wells believed that to be the case, given the situation she found you in at Spanish Camp. Ms. Wells believed that Icilda surprised you after you located the gems, shot you, and was about to take the gems and kill you when Ms. Wells came upon the two of you."

"Yes," I said, as loudly as I could.

"Ms. Wells said that after shooting Icilda, she bandaged your wound, gathered up most of the emeralds, and left you at Spanish Camp, intending to fly from Anegada on the VI Birds helicopter."

I nodded.

"And when she found the helicopter disabled, she hid near the airport until the following morning, when she could board the *Bomba Charger* to make her escape with Brooks's ill-gotten fortune. Or, I should say, most of his ill-gotten fortune. Rollie Stoutt found about four million dollars' worth of stones scattered around the well at Spanish Camp when he processed the crime scene."

DC Lane sighed heavily. "That is the substance of Ms. Wells's statement. As you confirm the circumstances of her killing of Icilda, I will recommend to the senior crown counsel that she not be charged with a crime for that act. Her actions appear to be clearly a matter of justifiable defense of a law enforcement officer in the course of his duties. She will probably spend the next two decades in Her Majesty's Prison for the felony theft and firearms charges in any event."

The DC paused as if expecting a response to this information but there was none to be made. He went on.

"There is one other item, Special Constable Creque. During the course of her statement, Ms. Wells described how she had seduced you in order to, as she put it, 'keep a close eye on the local cop' and learn any information that might be of benefit to her."

The intersection of the pea-green wall with the worn linoleum floor at the far corner of the hospital room suddenly seemed to need my attention. I stared hard at it and said nothing.

DC Lane made a gruff sound in his throat and gave a knowing toss of his great black head. "I see no particular relevance to that piece of information in the formal report of this matter. I doubt that it will appear in the final transcript of Ms. Wells's statement when the stenographer completes it."

I turned to the DC but he refused to meet my eyes, saying, "You have been through enough, Special Constable."

At that moment, Nurse Rowell appeared in the doorway, tapping her wristwatch with an insistent index finger. "Deputy Commissioner, Dr. Patel has asked that any visitors be limited to fifteen minutes so that Constable Creque gets adequate rest."

"Of course, nurse," the DC said, "just one minute more."

Nurse Rowell shot the DC a stern look the equal of any I had seen dispensed by the DC, gave her watch two more palpations, and retreated to the hall.

DC Lane drew close to me. "The commissioner and the prime minister have asked that I convey the nation's gratitude for your recovery of Brooks's cache of emeralds. When you have sufficiently recuperated from your injuries, you have been invited to attend a session of the Legislative Council. It is my understanding that you will receive a commendation from the council for your valor."

"But—" I managed.

"No buts, Special Constable Creque. Your tenacious efforts led to the solution of three major crimes, one of which occurred over forty years ago. Your actions also prevented the removal of the proceeds of that forty-year-old crime from our country. The single living perpetrator is now housed in Her Majesty's Prison. You are responsible for the recovery of over fifty million dollars of Her Majesty's funds, funds that can now be used for their original purpose of improving Anegada and the rest of the BVI. And you were wounded and nearly died in the process. You will attend the session of the Legislative Council and be deservedly honored."

"Yes, sir," I rasped. I know an order when I hear one.

"There is a final item, Constable. The recent events have made it evident that having only a special constable on Anegada does not provide an adequate Royal Virgin Islands Police Force presence there. The position of special constable on Anegada is therefore being eliminated. We need a fully commissioned police constable there now. The prime minister has earmarked a portion of the funds you recovered to train and equip a constable for the island."

So that was it. I was out of a job, but what could I expect after the way I had botched things up? It was a miracle it had turned out as well as it had.

"I have been instructed by the commissioner to offer you the position," the DC intoned solemnly. "And I am proud to do so. Had the commissioner offered the position to anyone else, I would have resigned from the RVIPF. You do not need to tell me if you want the position now. Take your time, and work on regaining your health. The job is waiting for you whenever you feel well enough."

And with that, Deputy Commissioner Howard T. Lane snapped to attention, fired a crisp salute—fingers together, palm out—in my direction, and strode from the room.

Epilogue

"It is a fine morning, Constable Creque," Nurse Rowell greeted me in a voice as sunny as the view from my window. "Another couple of days and Dr. Patel thinks you should be ready for discharge."

My physical recovery was going well, with no permanent damage anticipated from my now-healing wounds. My emotional recovery was about as could be expected. I had survived a first major test, a fifteen-minute visit from Kevin, Tamia, Madda, and Dada, with a minimum of tears. I suspect Dr. Patel had carefully coached them before allowing them to see me; even Kevin and Tamia had avoided questions and comments about the massive disruption I had caused in their innocent lives. I had mumbled a general apology, which was met by quick statements that no apology was needed and that I should concentrate on getting better. An explanation, my explanation, for what had occurred was mercifully deferred to another time.

Nurse Rowell popped a thermometer in my mouth and plumped the pillows on the bed, humming softly as she worked. I was sitting up in an armchair, facing toward the placid waters of Road Harbour. I had the two-bed ICU to myself, even though I suspect I was well enough to graduate to the general ward. Nurse Rowell had taken me on as her personal project, and, as the ICU was her domain, it was there I remained.

An orderly brought in a breakfast tray of bacon, eggs, broiled tomatoes, black coffee, and fresh guava juice and placed it on a small table before me. Finally back on solid food, I tucked into the meal with abandon; an IV bag of "parenteral nutrition solution" is no match for a rasher of bacon.

My bacony reverie was interrupted by a knock on the door frame behind me, followed by an Eton-Oxford-accented voice. "So, this is how the aristocracy lives, while the hoi polloi in the general ward are forced to subsist on oatmeal and cold tea."

I turned and there stood Anthony Wedderburn with a piratical twinkle in his blue eyes. His blond dreadlocks were gone, cut away to allow treatment of his head wounds. In their place he sported a wrap of bandages canted into a kind of rakish turban. A loose hospital gown and floppy cotton socks completed his outfit.

"Anthony, it is so good to see you! When you were airlifted from Anegada, I thought I might never see you again."

"I could say the same of you, old man. They told me of your exploits, wounded and clawing your way across the burning sands like a cinema legionnaire. It looks as if you are well on the mend, though."

"The doctor says I may be discharged in a couple days."

"Excellent! But it seems I will beat you to the punch. My physician wants a final look later this morning, and if all is well, I am back in the open air this afternoon." Anthony beamed.

"Anthony," I said. "I want to apologize to you for involving you in this mess. I had no idea it would put you in danger."

"Not to worry, Teddy. As the bard said, all's well that ends well. You could not have known what would happen. And it takes more than a crack on the bonce to put me down." Anthony's face clouded and he said, "I say, I am forgetting my manners. I came to see about your health but also to offer my condolences on . . . your recent loss."

"Thank you, Anthony, you are very kind," I began, and then stopped, overcome and unable to speak. The great emptiness I had begun to perceive these last few days reappeared, an emptiness I could feel, literally, inside my chest where my heart had been. I knew the heart was still there, doing its stoic beating work, but somehow it was there and gone at the same moment, a void in its place. I supposed the void was grief, but how could I grieve for Icilda, who had tried to kill me and nearly succeeded? Icilda, who had betrayed me. Icilda, whom I had betrayed. I told myself I had some sorting out to do.

A wry smile touched the corners of my mouth. "The loss

isn't that recent, Anthony. It happened a long time ago. I guess I just wasn't able to admit it to myself."

Anthony made no response. There is no response to be made when such words are spoken. I broke the silence.

"What about you, Anthony? What's next for you?"

"I am thinking, Teddy, that the blow to the head did me some good." De White Rasta smiled. "That and the spot of work I did for you on the coded notebook. It made me realize that there is something more to life than stumbling stoned through the day and finding a warm spot to crash each night. To answer your question, I intend to go home, settle down, and try to find some good work to do. I'm not sure what just yet but I know it will come to me."

"Home? To England?" I asked.

"England?" Anthony was momentarily puzzled. "No, home to Anegada, of course. What about you, Teddy?"

I turned to the window. Outside, a sailboat skimmed across Road Harbour. In the near distance, a pair of mockingbirds frolicked in the branches of a soursop tree. The trade wind freshened, cutting the heat out of the morning. The world, and life, went on.

Off to the northeast, too low to be seen from Tortola, my world, the Drowned Land named by Columbus, went on as well. The sunrise at the East End; my two lovely children; the salt ponds; Dada and Madda; the pink sands and long sweep of Cow Wreck Bay; The Settlement, filled with friends more like family; the bustle and excitement of the *Bomba Charger* arriving at the government dock; the lonely beauty of the flats;

all went on. The sorting out I needed would be the work of many days, but I sensed it had begun. And I knew where it would be completed.

“I’ll be going home, too,” I said.

Acknowledgments

The experience of a first novel has shown me that the writer has one of the smaller parts in the work that reaches the public. The list of those whose inspiration, support, efforts, and encouragement deserve thanks comprises almost everyone whose life has touched mine, and is impossible to record here. You know who you are and you have my gratitude.

Special thanks to friend, fellow writer, and first reader Ed Duncan, who urged me to continue after reading my manuscript. Without your encouragement, this story would be sitting in a desk drawer somewhere, unread.

My appreciation also to beta readers Dick (Spike) Spicer and Larry Boudon for your sensible comments and sharp eyes.

Thanks to the Mystery Writers of America and St. Martin's Minotaur for sponsoring the competition that led to the publication of this book and for their willingness to give a chance to those of us who travel without an agent or a pedigree.

My abiding gratitude to Andy Martin, Kelley Ragland, and the entire team at Minotaur Books for transforming my rough manuscript into the polished and professional-looking book the reader sees today.

To Elizabeth Lacks, my incomparable editor, a special place in my heart for your patience in guiding a sixty-year-old rookie through the editing and publishing process. You are the best.

My appreciation to the precise and insightful Aja Pollock, copy editor extraordinaire.

For their warm and welcoming ways, thanks to the people of Anegada and the British Virgin Islands.

For teaching their son that there are no limits, thanks to my parents, Alma and Lee Keyse.

Last but most important, thanks to my dear wife, Irene, who believed when others did not, who encouraged when others would not, and who made me a better writer and a better man.